Some Other Way

by

Margot Johnson

Some Other Way

Cover Art by *The Wild Rose Press, Inc.*

The Wild Rose Press, Inc.
PO Box 708
Adams Basin, NY 14410-0708
Visit us at www.thewildrosepress.com

Publishing History
First Edition, 2024
Trade Paperback ISBN 978-1-5092-5381-4
Digital ISBN 978-1-5092-5382-1

Published in the United States of America

"Jump in before I take more than my share." He patted his stomach. "Got to keep my boyish figure."

Jayne slapped a hand to her mouth and laughed. "I think you missed your chance. But you can delude yourself."

"He's a man after my own heart." Tasha tapped a hand on each ample hip.

"Ouch!" Evan exaggerated a mock sad face. He could stand to lose a few pounds, but he didn't worry about his size. Jayne would forgive a less-than-perfect physique, wouldn't she? Food served as a good antidote for loneliness and boredom, and it just plain tasted good.

"Don't pout." Jayne glanced over her shoulder. "I can't stand a whiner."

"Hey, it's my party, and I'll whine if I want to." He grinned and sang a few bars, butchering the lyrics.

She snapped back her gaze. Eyebrows raised, she shook her head.

He knew exactly how to get a strong reaction.

Tasha giggled. "I can't wait to hear you sing at campfire."

"I can wait…forever." Jayne crinkled her nose.

Her eyes sparkled with fun, and her cheeks shaded pink from the wind. Hair drawn back in a sleek ponytail, she wore blue jeans, hiking boots, and a quilted jacket. Casual and outdoorsy, her style blended with the crowd yet grabbed his attention.

Would he ever draw her into a tender hug? For an instant, attraction squashed the air from his lungs. How would his lips feel brushing her cheeks, her forehead, and her lips?

Praise

"I loved *Let it Snowball*. Margot Johnson has a way of making a festive atmosphere seem very real. Combine that with a warm and gentle love story that feels truly authentic, and you have a winner of a story."

~ *Mary Balogh, New York Times Bestselling Author*

~*~

"The author shines at bringing family dynamics to life with all of their love and imperfections."

~ *Donna Gartshore, Love Inspired Author*

~*~

Love Takes Flight "will set your heart beating and your fingers crossing as you hope for the very best ending…it is a lovely introduction to Canada."

~ *Annette Bower, Award-winning Contemporary Romance Author*

~*~

"*Let it Simmer* is a funny, cute, and romantic story."

~*Michelle Godard-Richer, Author*

Dedication

For Katie & Carolyn ~
because family means the world

Acknowledgments

One of the themes in *Some Other Way* is motherhood, and being a mom is one of my greatest joys in life.

Thank you, Laura and Lindsay, for making it such a fun and fulfilling journey.

Thank you, Alyssa, for showing me how a birth mother can love and stay involved in her child's life after she chooses open adoption.

Thank you, Mom, for setting a great example.

Thank you, Rick, for always being there for me…and our whole family.

Thank you to my editor, Leanne Morgena, and The Wild Rose Press team for helping bring my sixth book into the world. It's another dream come true!

Finally, a big thank you to all my readers. I love hearing from you. Please send me a note or post a review.

Chapter 1

A pink balloon popped, and Jayne jumped. Overhead, a tangle of pastel streamers rustled and swayed. As surrogate auntie, she wouldn't dream of missing this party. She gathered a jumble of wrapping paper off the floor and organized gifts into a neat pile on the carpet in a corner of the sunny, spacious living room. Giggles and shrieks rang over the sounds of bouncy kids' dance music. Cara was a very lucky girl.

Today's celebration offered Jayne a welcome reprieve from the stresses of a looming issue at work. She rested her gaze on the birthday girl and her friends, all skipping and twirling fancy dresses. Instantly, regret wound tight as a ribbon around her heart. Much as she loved sharing Cara's fifth birthday party—and all the special events in her life—she nursed an achy blend of joy and sorrow. Even when she busied her hands tidying the room, she couldn't stop them from quivering.

Blinking to clear the mist from her eyes, she clutched a piece of tissue and inhaled a shaky breath. With its tasteful, neutral furnishings and colorful, original artwork, the home of Cara's parents, Dr. Brad and Mallory Lewis, was as warm and welcoming as the compassionate couple. The air swirled as sweet as candy around the girls' flushed faces and lively dance moves. Cara's brown hair swished, and blunt bangs hung straight as a sheet, just like Jayne's. Her hazel eyes glittered behind oval, pink glasses perched on her little snub nose.

"Thanks for your help." Smiling, Mallory surveyed the constant motion. "Cara and her friends never stop, but I don't mind."

"Thank you for including me in the fun." Arms extended, Jayne spun once to imitate the girls. She never doubted Mallory treasured every moment with Cara. Sometimes, Jayne envied her so much her chest and throat squeezed until she almost couldn't breathe. She wanted to hate Mallory. But, of course, no one could ever dislike Mallory, with her impossibly kind and generous heart and her equally nice husband, Brad. They did everything possible to make Jayne feel like one of the family.

The couple's shining qualities were the precise reason Jayne trusted them from the moment she interviewed them five-and-a-half years ago and then finalized a private adoption. She gave up her beautiful daughter on the condition she would always remain involved in Cara's life.

"In a few minutes, we'll calm the whirlwind and steer the little princesses to the table for cake." Mallory smiled again and flashed perfect, white teeth. "Too bad the weather didn't cooperate for a yard party." She flipped her head from side to side, bouncing her blonde curls.

Strangers must wonder where Cara—Jayne's little look-alike—inherited her ordinary hair compared to her mom's vibrant halo and her dad's reddish tinge. "My dad always says, 'If you don't like the weather, wait a few minutes.' " Shrugging, Jayne glanced across the hubbub in the room and out the front window. In some years, October first in Prairieville, a small town in the Canadian prairies, shone as warm as the day Cara was born. Unfortunately, today, a chilly wind whipped crisp, brown leaves across the neighborhood and foreshadowed colder days ahead. Only Jayne's golden retriever, Sally, embraced the cold and scrounged the backyard for squirrels.

"Okay, girls. Time to tiptoe like ballerinas." Brad held up his phone camera to capture party highlights and winked at Jayne and Mallory. "Think that idea will calm them?"

"Smart." Jayne chuckled, and her momentary pain dissolved. She really couldn't imagine better parents for Cara. Mallory and Brad gave her everything a girl needed—a loving family, a warm home, and gentle guidance. If only Jayne had made better choices, then everything would be different.

Instead, she pined for a child of her own someday and threw her energy and passion into her work at Adopt-a-Dog, rescuing abused and abandoned dogs. They needed her, and she needed them just as much. Jayne straightened, tossed a ball of tissue into a garbage bag, and clapped to the music. Despite her intermittent pain, she embraced every moment with Cara.

Normally, her parents would attend the party, too, sharing in the fun and vying for Cara's attention. Jayne would never admit the truth, but she was glad they were away on vacation and unable to attend. They loved Cara like a granddaughter, but sometimes, their presence reminded Jayne of the guilt and shame she tried to shed like a scratchy wool sweater.

The doorbell rang, and Brad cocked his head

toward the front door. "Must be Evan. I'll answer." He dropped his phone into his pocket.

"Evan who?" Jayne stiffened. An unpleasant memory prickled her back, and she scrunched another wad of wrapping paper with a satisfying crackle. The only Evan she knew moved to Toronto after high school, and he belonged over two thousand kilometers away.

"Twirl like me, Auntie Jayne." Cara motioned with both hands and demonstrated.

Jayne tipped forward onto her toes. "I like your spin better." She was the furthest thing from a ballerina. Her feet belonged firmly planted on the ground.

"Now try this, Auntie Jayne." Cara swooped into a deep bend and nearly lost her balance.

"Beautiful." Jayne clapped and glanced toward the door. Would Brad invite the visitor to join the party?

Mallory brushed Jayne's forearm. "Evan Scott is the new doctor who came to expand the medical clinic." Laughing, she swept a hand across the chaotic scene. "If he wants a slower pace, he chose the wrong place."

Jayne adjusted the zipper on her sweater. Underneath, trepidation whirled in an unpleasant dance. He was *that* Evan, the blond-haired, blue-eyed guy who crushed her heart. If he intended to expand the medical clinic, he meant trouble for her and Adopt-a-Dog. No surprise. He never could be trusted. Well, she wasn't a meek teenager anymore. She'd show him she was no pushover.

Mallory placed her palms over her ears. "How can five little girls make so much noise?" She tapped Cara's shoulder and put a finger to her lips in a gentle signal to lower her volume.

Cara complied for a full three seconds, then echoed her friends' squeals.

Brad opened the door, and chilly air whooshed into the living room.

Jayne shivered, as much from the arrival of Evan as the temperature. She hunched her shoulders and shrank into the background.

"Come in, if you dare." Mallory drew him into the room.

"Wow." Evan stepped back. "Looks like I crashed a party. I won't stay long. I'm assembling furniture, and somehow, I lost my drill in the move. Brad said I could borrow one."

Brad crinkled his eyes into a smile. "I'll grab it. Wait a minute."

"I think you know our friend, Jayne." Smiling, Mallory waved her forward.

Flitting her gaze up and down, she'd recognize him anywhere. Of average height, he still sported curly, fair hair. His eyes still peered with intensity, and his lips stretched wide to reveal shiny, white teeth. He had filled out from the lanky kid she once knew into a solid, muscular physique. If he hadn't changed, his self-confidence and sense of humor drew people into his circle.

Long ago, Jane agreed with Mallory and Brad most people didn't need details of their close relationship. Not everyone approved of Jayne's past or her decision to give up a child yet stay involved in her life. "Hello." Jayne squished her lips together in an awkward, close-mouthed smile. She flipped her gaze to Evan's face, and heat crept to her cheekbones. Her heartbeats sped faster than the upbeat music in the background.

"Jayne Jones? Of course, we know each other." He jerked back his head and widened his enormous, blue eyes. "Long time no see. I didn't know you still lived in Prairieville." Eyes slightly magnified, he peered through lenses with trendy frames and stuck out a hand. "Nice to see you again."

Jayne paused, extended a firm hand, and recoiled from the warmth skipping up her arm. "Welcome back." She couldn't pretend she was glad to see him. As soon as possible, without seeming totally rude, she'd scurry to the kitchen and add candles to the birthday cake. Anything to escape his unsettling presence. She hadn't seen him in fifteen years, and after all this time, her heartbeats shouldn't patter like she lived in the throes of a high school crush. Her mouth dried, and she licked her lips, keeping them carefully folded inward to conceal her teeth. He didn't need to notice her front teeth still crossed at the corner tips, a flaw in her appearance her mother never let her forget.

Relaxing his shoulders now that he was in from the chilly air, Evan blinked and studied her. "I thought you left town."

"I did." Jayne racked her brain for something clever or witty to say. "For a while. Most of our class left after grad, but I came back…like the cat."

"Clever." Evan picked up on her song reference and snapped his fingers in time to an imaginary soundtrack. He laughed. "But not the very next day."

Evan still liked to joke. Maybe she'd momentarily diverted him from questioning her reasons for leaving or returning. She didn't intend to elaborate, and anyway, he probably wasn't interested. The less she said, the less she'd feel pressured to share. Clenching

6

her jaw, she drew in a deep breath.

"Were you two high school sweethearts?" Mallory flipped her gaze from Jayne to Evan.

"Ask her." Evan grinned and pointed at Jayne.

Jayne froze. He was as confident and annoying as ever. "Uh…" Any explanation caught in her throat. She wouldn't give him the satisfaction of knowing how much he meant back then. She huffed and rolled her eyes. "Hardly." In her dreams. Turned out, he just used her brains, but she never forgot him.

"I just felt a stab." Laughing, he thumped a fist on his chest.

"Hmmm…sounds like some history there." Smiling, Mallory widened her eyes. "You should get together for coffee sometime and catch up." She glanced at Jayne. "Evan owns a golden retriever, too."

"Yep." Evan tilted his head toward the door. "Dudley's waiting out front. I told him to sit and stay. He listens pretty well."

"Cute name." Jayne responded through narrowed lips and forced a close-mouthed smile. His plaid, flannel jacket and faded blue jeans struck the right note of casual and outdoorsy.

"Yeah, it suits him." Evan chuckled. "He's too much of a person and too goofy to wear a typical dog name."

"Same with Sally." Her dog was a steady friend and good company for a single person living in her own small house. Sally demonstrated how the right surroundings and love could restore an animal to good health and a happy life.

"Here you go, sir." Brad reappeared with a drill.

The interruption saved Jayne from responding to

Mallory's suggestion she and Evan should reconnect.

"See you at the office Monday." Brad handed over the tool. "Between patients, we can talk about expansion plans."

Apprehension tingled up Jayne's back. Her suspicions were correct. Evan returned to Prairieville to expand the medical clinic and snatch away her dream for Adopt-a-Dog. She harbored her own vision for the open parcel of land adjacent to both services.

"Better run." Evan grabbed the doorknob. "Dudley and furniture assembly await." He raised the drill in a half wave, then glanced at Jayne. "I'll get your contact info from Brad and give you a call."

Jayne stiffened, stared, and blinked. The bouncy party music filled in the airspace and covered her speechless response. Was he oblivious to her less-than-enthusiastic reaction?

Evan spun and hurried out the door.

He owned a golden retriever, so he must possess some redeeming qualities, but owning a cute dog didn't mean she'd agree to meet him for coffee. He intended to grab the property she desperately needed to expand Adopt-a-Dog. Sure, he worked as a big-time doctor and all, but he'd hurt her before, and she wouldn't give him the chance to do it again.

****

At the end of his first day working alongside Brad at the Prairieville Medical Clinic, Evan stretched and removed his patterned lab coat. Today it was decorated with a parade of cartoon characters. Tomorrow, the design might display dogs and cats or stripes. Patients of all ages—not only children—responded well to his collection of whimsical jackets, taking their minds off their health worries. He had juggled a full schedule all day and treated a steady stream of patients.

Wagging his thick tail, Dudley wandered in from the reception area. He filled a new job, too, as office greeter.

"Good boy." Evan bent and rewarded his dog with a vigorous rub and a quick scratch behind the ears.

Shedding his conservative, white lab coat, Brad appeared in the doorway. "The day flew by, and we didn't talk about expansion plans. Tomorrow, let's make sure we meet. I'd like to fast-track the project."

"Sounds good." Excitement flickered in Evan's chest. The vision of a large, multi-purpose healthcare center had sold him on the opportunity here in Prairieville. Behind Brad, the stark, white walls shouted clean and boring—not at all the image Evan preferred. Sure, sterility ranked as the utmost importance, but that requirement didn't mean they couldn't have a little fun with the décor. Over time, he'd add colorful artwork and more toys for kids. Bringing Dudley to the clinic— as long as patients with allergies didn't react—was a good first step.

"Anything planned for the evening?" Brad tossed the garment in a laundry bin.

"Not much." Evan straightened and smothered a yawn. "Still a few boxes left to unpack. Long walk with Dudley." He shifted and jingled a couple of loonies, Canadian dollar coins, in his pocket. Then he joined hands behind his back and raised them in an arc to create a deeper stretch to ease the cramps in his shoulders. He healed his patients' pains all the time, but nothing eased the gnawing emptiness he carried in his heart. Work filled his days, but evenings and weekends emphasized the hole inside.

"Why don't you grab a quick supper and join me at the youth group?" Brad scrubbed his hands at the sink near the examination rooms. "Mallory takes Cara to the kids' club at the rec center, and I help with the teen program. Tonight is games night." He dried his hands. "C'mon, it'll be fun."

"I, uh, don't know." Evan shifted his gaze to Dudley.

The dog wagged his tail, tilted his head, and gently woofed.

Dudley acted as if he agreed with Brad's suggestion. Evan wasn't so sure. Maybe some kids looked up to a doctor, but what else could he offer? He didn't even know his true identity. The hole inside him gaped, then constricted into a heavy lump of lingering rejection by his birth mother and his ex-wife, Bethany.

"You don't need experience to join." Brad flipped a jacket over his shoulders and flicked off the lights. "Come to the flat, green building at the end of Prairie Drive. Bring Dudley. The kids will love him."

"I'll see." Evan was not about to commit on the spot. Sinking onto the couch and switching on a movie sounded just fine. He wouldn't have to act *on,* joking and laughing to match the face he constantly presented. He'd think about it over a hamburger and salad but doubted he'd accept Brad's invitation. "Thanks for the offer. Let's go, Dudley."

Evan's rented house waited just a few blocks down the street. Hunching his shoulders, he gripped the office doorknob and braced himself for a wind gust. He couldn't anticipate a warm greeting by a loving family like Brad's, but at least, he had his loyal, canine companion for company. Outside, the air whisked the crisp, dry scent of autumn.

Brad followed Evan out the door, checked the lock, and paused. The sun, low in the sky, sent a weak light across his face. "You'll meet Jayne there. She volunteers with the teenage girls. Usually, her dog comes, too." He arched his eyebrows.

At Brad's teasing, Evan's face heated—much warmer than the cool air should allow. Jayne wasn't the prettiest or most outgoing woman he'd ever met, but she was cute in a quiet way and, apparently, single. Her eyes reminded him of a frightened fawn, and a vague memory of an unpleasant incident circled at the edge of his mind. Even so, getting reacquainted wouldn't hurt, would it?

Chapter 2

"Jaynie?"

"Hi, Mom." Standing in the kitchen of her small bungalow, Jayne glanced at her fitness tracker to check the time. Her parents had been vacationing in Vancouver for just one week, and already, she had heard from Mom five times.

"I called to share some exciting news."

"Oh? The youth group starts soon, so I can't talk for long." Shadowed by a wagging Sally, Jayne paced from the kitchen to the living room.

She loved her compact, tidy home. The kitchen glowed white and bright with red accents, just the way *Home Style* magazine showcased. Pausing, she surveyed the living room. Leather loveseats and coordinating chairs in shades of tan camouflaged the ever-present dog hair. Red toss cushions, scented candles, and colorful artwork created flow between the rooms. She glanced out the front window and, in the fading light, watched leaves skitter across the driveway. Autumn had arrived.

"First things first. I miss you. So does your dad."

"I miss you, too, Mom." Jayne squeezed the phone, and a river of guilt trickled from her words to her chest. A tiny white lie wouldn't hurt, would it? Much as she loved her mother, she despised her overbearing presence. Escaping Mom's grip had changed the course of Jayne's life, and she'd never forget her failings. The evidence lived in Cara and in Mom's constant reminders.

"I hope you and Dad are having fun." Jayne retraced her steps to the kitchen and, with one hand, loaded the dishwasher and kicked the door shut. If she kept moving, she'd sidestep Mom's words before they trapped her in a corner. She took a deep breath. "I don't want to be late. Maybe you can share your news another time." Tomorrow evening, she'd attend the town council meeting, so she might miss Mom's call. She rubbed her chest where a prickle of guilt and exasperation collided.

"How was Cara's birthday party? I'm so sad we missed it, considering the fact she's nearly a true granddaughter. Sometimes, I almost forget the unhappy circumstances of her birth."

Mom's voice tilted downward like it was yanked by a frown. Jayne pictured her thick bottom lip forced outward and her narrowed eyes drooping at the corners. She never had to wonder what Mom thought about anything. Instantly, shame and regret circled in Jayne's stomach, and she inhaled deep breaths until the unpleasant feeling dissolved. She treasured dear Cara, and she already battled enough conflicted emotions without Mom loading on more.

"The birthday girl enjoyed lots of fun. When you get home, you'll hear all the details." Shoulders tensing, Jayne glanced again at the time, opened a closet door, and snapped on Sally's leash. If she didn't leave soon, she'd be late. Even now, she'd need to jog the six blocks to the rec center. "I better say goodbye."

"No, Jaynie. Listen to my news."

"You'll have to wait, Mom." How typical of Mom to discount Jayne's feelings. She choked back irritation so she didn't lash out.

"Do *not* hang up on me."

Her mom's tone smacked Jayne into silence.

"I'll speak quickly."

Jayne held a finger poised to end the call. "Not now, Mom. I'm late for the youth group." She stomped a foot.

Sally flinched, but the noise didn't travel over the airwaves to interrupt Mom.

"Aunt Patsy wants to pay for orthodontic work to straighten your teeth. I'm thrilled! Why she didn't think of the idea sooner, I do not know. But after all these years of seeing you talk and smile like you have glue on your lips, I know you'll accept her generous offer. Think about it. I'll let you go now. Bye-bye, dear." Mom clicked off the call.

Jayne lifted her glasses and swiped at her eyes. She swallowed, then guzzled a glass of water to cool the burning embers in her throat. Trust Mom to remind her she remained plain Jayne, an unwed mother with a shameful past. No one else made her feel as remorseful, unattractive, and inadequate.

When Jayne was younger, she heard Mom label her a beautiful girl, but she knew the truth. Mom didn't believe her own words, or why would she have instructed Jayne to smile with her mouth closed? Why would Evan have insulted her in front of the whole, grade twelve English class? He probably didn't even remember the day he swung backward in his seat to ask her how to spell the word *anomaly*. His talking to her was an anomaly in itself.

Evan had smirked and delivered his punch line in an exaggerated whisper so everyone could hear. "Jayne's *teeth* are an anomaly."

Maybe he hadn't meant to hurt her, but even now, all these years later, his words left a singed spot inside her chest. She should have known right then she could never trust him, and she should never have given him a second chance.

She shook her head and bit her lip. She wouldn't worry about ancient history. "C'mon, Sal Gal, let's go." Jayne squatted and let her gentle golden retriever lick her cheek. Sally accepted her, no matter what. She fondled the dog's velvety ears, straightened, and hurried from the warmth of home into the chilly evening.

Practically sprinting to the rec center and inhaling huge mouthfuls of clean, prairie air, Jayne shook away the tension in her arms and legs. Mostly, she managed the veiled criticism her mother doled out. Mom fixated on physical flaws, the circumstances of Cara's birth, and anything else that bothered her. Over the years, Jayne had accepted that the ache in her heart—the kind no painkiller could touch—never fully eased.

Slowing in front of a grayish-green building, she climbed the rec center steps and paused before she greeted the girls inside. On the heels of her latest encounter with Mom, she searched deep for steady confidence and a positive outlook.

She was ready. Every week, she met with teenage girls who wanted to volunteer for community service, talk about personal challenges, or just socialize with their peers. No matter the reason, Jayne strived to be their friend, teacher, and mentor. After a brief welcome, this evening's agenda focused on pure fun.

Opening the door, she sniffed the familiar scent of polished floor tile. She paused for a moment to slow her heart rate and drink in the autumn foliage and orange pumpkins adorning the lobby area. On the main level, activity rooms for meetings and classes branched off a main hallway. From downstairs, laughter and the murmur of conversation echoed up the stairwell. With Sally still by her side, Jayne spun toward the gathering below.

With a bang, the front door blew shut, and the last person Jayne expected to see arrived in a whirl of cool air. She stiffened her cheeks and shook her hair into place. Why were Evan Scott and his dog here now, where they, most definitely, did not belong?

"Hi, Jayne. Sit, Dudley." Evan peered around and glanced at the stairs.

"Hi, Evan. This is Sally." She rubbed her dog's head. Oh, wow. Now they performed dog introductions. The situation felt even more awkward than yesterday's encounter.

"Pleased to meet you, Sally." Evan held out his hand for Sally to sniff.

Sally sat and raised a paw.

Chuckling, Evan shook Sally's paw and let Dudley rub noses with his newfound friend.

"They probably think they caught a reflection." At the sight of the two, nearly identical pups, Jayne couldn't help but smile wide enough her teeth must partly show. Regaining control, she drew her lips together again. "Are you lost?"

"Maybe. I'm not sure. If so, it won't be the first time." Evan grimaced and shifted his gaze in an exaggerated searching motion in all directions.

Jayne allowed him a couple of closed-mouth noises that were supposed to be a polite "ha" but, to her ears, sounded like she cleared her throat. Choked with discomfort, she peered through her glasses and struggled to understand. Why did his gregarious response feel forced? Could this self-assured man truly feel lost—not in direction but in a deeper, more significant way? "C'mon, I'll show you where to go." Jayne, trailed by Sally, led the way down the stairs toward the noisy lower level.

"I'm used to direction." With Dudley by his side, Evan followed. "People tell me where to go all the time." Feet thudding on the steps, he chuckled.

Jayne rolled her eyes and didn't joke back. His crack reminded her too much of his inconsiderate, high-school humor—something she'd rather forget. "This is Friendship Hall." Breathing in the slightly musty, basement smell, she halted in the doorway and surveyed the large, open area ahead. After last year's facelift, the walls gleamed cream with motivational quotes stenciled along the ceiling. The taupe, laminate flooring stretched ready to weather a pounding from hundreds of feet. Right now, it was being tested with traffic from groupings of kids of all ages.

"Welcome to the youth group." With a flourish, Jayne flung an arm across the lively scene before them. Voices and laughter floated over the space. Glancing at Evan, she choked back a giggle. He retracted like he was afraid to step off a curb into oncoming traffic. Apparently, the floor wouldn't be the only thing tested this evening. Evan might have met his match.

****

"Sit and stay." Evan put a hand in front of his dog's nose to emphasize the instructions, even though most times, he was quick to obey.

"Go see the kids." Jayne clicked off Sally's leash. "Let Dudley go, too."

"Okay." Evan released Dudley and watched his retriever lope toward the action. Definitely, Brad had not prepared him for the youth group.

Kids of all ages milled, ran, and fidgeted, all talking and laughing with friends in a noisy blur.

Evan had pictured a bunch of lively teens but not an all-out carousel that made him dizzy. He worked with kids as patients all the time, but nothing prepared him for leading a large group. Oh well, he liked action, so bring it on.

"Hey, man. You made it." Running a hand over his spiky, carroty hair, Brad hustled over.

"Yeah, let the fun begin." Evan unzipped his jacket and planted hands on hips.

"Auntie Jayne." Cara threw her arms around Jayne's thighs.

Brad tipped his head toward the pair. "Cara is so close to Jayne she calls her Auntie."

Evan nodded. Across the room, he spotted Mallory, gathering the younger kids into a group.

Mallory glanced over her shoulder and waved at Cara.

Catching Evan totally off guard, he fought a rush of loneliness clutching his throat. He shifted and breathed in the happy commotion, but the heavy sensation radiating from his throat to his chest only grew. Why did he feel even more alone when he was in a crowd, especially next to a happy couple like Mallory and Brad? His new business partner and wife had everything he wished for, including a beautiful child.

Taking a deep breath and plastering on a wide smile, he refocused his gaze on Jayne and Brad. "Thanks for the heads-up." Evan jabbed in Brad's direction with an elbow. "You said, 'Come to the youth group.' You didn't say the zoo." The room smelled like old running shoes and teenage grooming products, propelling him back fifteen years to his own high school days.

"I wanted to entice you here and not scare you off." Grinning, Brad dodged the motion. "Trust me. The chaos is not as bad as it looks."

"Hi, Cara. Did you have a good day at kindergarten?" Jayne drew the little girl close and squatted to face her.

Cara nodded and straightened her pink glasses. A moment before, when she pressed her face into Jayne's stomach, she had knocked them wonky.

Jayne kissed a finger and placed it on the tip of Cara's little nose.

Her love for the little girl radiated like the sun. The glow made Jayne even prettier than he remembered.

Grinning at Jayne, Cara giggled.

"Have lots and lots of fun at your kids' club tonight." Straightening, Jayne glanced at Brad. "Time to start?"

Cara skipped away.

With their thin limbs, straight hair, and round glasses, the little girl and Jayne looked more alike than Cara and her parents. Sometimes, genetics surprised and puzzled even a doctor. Did he resemble either of his parents? He had no idea whatsoever. He'd never met or seen a picture of either. Regret thumped across his torso. From the start, they never cared to share his life in any way. The truth hurt, even though his adoptive mom assured him they loved him.

"Yep, ready if you are." Brad wound to the center of the room, raised an arm, and waited in silence until the kids noticed and followed suit.

At the far end of the room, Mallory led the younger children out a door to another area of the building.

Panting near the kids, Dudley slowed his wagging tail, sat, and stared at Brad.

Sally groaned and flopped onto the floor.

Brad's control was impressive. Within minutes, the hubbub quieted, and everyone listened for instructions. A skilled doctor, devoted husband, caring dad, and now, expert youth leader, Brad really did have it all. Inside Evan, envy crawled next to loneliness and leaned on his already heavy chest. Venturing here tonight might have been a mistake.

"Let's join the group." Jayne waved him toward the hub of the room.

Did she sense the situation tested his confidence? Here in a group of people who shared strong bonds, he didn't quite fit. He'd muster his go-to joking manner and connect with the kids soon enough, but for a few minutes, at least, he needed to breathe and convince his body to chill. He enjoyed reading medical journals more than interacting with groups of mostly strangers. "You know how to rock a Monday night." Evan glanced sideways at Jayne. She scanned the room, showing no sign she felt his gaze rest on her profile.

In an instant, he flashed back to high school and transformed her into the modest, smart girl who grabbed his interest. He had only hinted at his attraction before he teased and cajoled her into writing a major English essay he needed to complete the class. All these years later, she was still modestly nice-looking in a studious way. Her precise bangs just grazed her eyebrows, and her neat hair swung somewhere between her chin and her shoulders. According to the posters in the hair salons in Toronto, a stylist would probably call it a bob. Horn-rimmed glasses nicely framed her hazel eyes. Even her uneven front teeth were kind of cute, although he seldom spotted them behind her awkward, close-mouthed smiles. Teeth didn't need to stand in a perfect line. Not everybody wanted or could afford orthodontics.

"First up is dodgeball." Brad raised his voice. "But before we start, I'll introduce my friend, Evan. He's the new doctor in town."

Evan raised a hand in greeting. Was he cool enough to hang out here? Maybe he'd keep his mind off the emptiness following him everywhere like Dudley.

"I need two volunteers to grab the balls out of the storage room." Brad pointed at a boy and a girl.

The pair jogged away.

Evan could handle dodgeball. Shoving his hands into the pockets of his jeans, he shuffled to one side of the room.

In the center, Brad divided the group into teams.

"You come here every week?" Evan swivelled toward a teenage boy, sporting dark, asymmetrical hair, large, white teeth, and a mild case of acne.

"Yeah, pretty much." The boy shifted and stared at his feet. "We do different activities and talk about stuff…things our parents don't know."

"Sounds good. When I was your age, I joined a youth group, mostly because my parents forced me."

The boy snapped his head upright and widened his eyes.

Evan had made a mistake. He'd keep the conversation to the game and not plant ideas in kids' heads over whether coming here was a good idea or not. "I'm Evan. Your name is…?"

"Tyler."

"Pleased to meet you, Tyler. Play much dodgeball?"

"A bit." Tyler studied the floor. He stubbed a toe, and the rubber squeaked.

"Yeah? Not me." Evan slapped his hands together and rubbed them the same way he scrubbed between patients. "But I'm ready."

"What about you?" Evan tipped his head toward a girl with arms crossed and one hip stuck out. "Ever play?"

"Never." She shook her head and swished her golden ponytail. "Mostly, I come here to talk to Jayne. She's awesome."

"Oh?" Evan quirked an eyebrow. He'd like to know more about Jayne, and this girl might enlighten him.

"Yeah, she teaches me a lot." She shrugged. "You know…girl stuff. Things I wonder, but my mom doesn't tell me."

No, he didn't exactly know, but whatever Jayne shared with the girls seemed to make an impact. She must have some deep insights and life experience to offer, and maybe she was a trusted confidante. Even in their brief interactions, he sensed she offered something deep. Somehow, he read in her face she'd experienced things that weren't easy. The slight downward dip at the outer corners of her eyes, probably too subtle for most to notice, hinted at sorrow. "Right on. We can all use a friend like Jayne." Evan definitely could. A person couldn't count on just anyone to offer support when needed. He'd long ago decided not to let himself feel that disappointment ever again.

He scanned the group and spotted Jayne on the opposite side. He caught her gaze for an instant, and uneasiness readjusted his insides like they played their own game of dodgeball. She was a mature woman and no longer the shy teen he toyed with years ago. On the surface an ordinary woman, she sparked his senses in a way he hadn't felt in a very long time. Soon, he could blame the rush of heat up his neck on the physical activity.

After Brad's quick review of the rules, he whistled the start of the game, and balls flew in all directions.

Evan stretched sideways, and a ball missed him by inches. He grabbed the ball and launched a high toss.

A boy jumped over the bounce.

Laughing, Evan ducked and scooted away. Then *smack*. A ball hit him on the back of the head so hard it knocked off his glasses. They landed with a loud *clack* on the hard surface. He heard, more than saw, the lenses shatter beyond repair.

Brad blew the whistle to stop the action.

Evan dropped to his knees and groped on the floor for what was left of his glasses. He was nearly blind without them, so he could only detect a blur of color and a murmur of voices.

"Oops. I'm very sorry, Evan. I owe you a new pair

of glasses."

From out of the fog, a familiar voice quivered with a mix of apology and amusement. He squinted and deciphered a very hazy Jayne, clapping a hand over her mouth. Evan let loose a giant laugh to break the tension and show everyone he didn't hold a grudge.

The group joined in.

"I'll pick up the pieces." Jayne dove forward.

"No problem. Dudley can serve as my guide dog." Straightening, Evan sensed the atmosphere relax." Not that he could discern Jayne's facial expression, but he could imagine her eyes lighting and her lips stretched over her teeth in a partial, awkward smile. He couldn't wait to see her clearly again. The incident offered a great excuse to meet—the sooner the better—and assure her he was okay. But would Jayne agree?

Chapter 3

The next morning, Jayne arrived with Sally at Adopt-a-Dog, poured coffee, and plunked onto her desk chair. She swung to face her employee and friend, Tasha, at the work station across the office.

As always, Tasha's funky style contrasted with Jayne's understated appearance. Today, she wore her frizzy, black hair tied into a wiry puff on the top of her head. A red sweater patterned with gold beads set off her dark complexion.

With a busy day ahead, Jayne would get down to business shortly, but first, she'd steal a few minutes to chitchat. She had a lot to share.

The muffled yips of dogs and murmured comments floated from the back kennel area, where workers already attended to the dogs. A door and limited soundproofing couldn't contain all the noise from drifting into the office space. She breathed in the musky smell permeating the building, even though the kennel received frequent cleaning. Cats and other small animals were housed in a different facility in the next town over.

"Did you see Cara last night?" Tasha set down her coffee mug. "I bought you a treat." She passed a bakery bag.

Even with her ample hips, Tasha didn't worry about what she ate. The delicious aroma of sugar and cinnamon wafted. "Yum. Thank you." Jayne's mouth watered. "Yes, on her way to the kids' club." She pictured Cara's earnest, little face and placed a hand on her stomach to still the quiver that persisted whenever she mentioned the precious child's name.

"And?" Tasha leaned forward. "How did you feel?"

"Much better than on her birthday. It's the toughest day of the year." Jayne winced and rubbed her middle. "I was mostly at peace, but a little achy…and a little—I hate to admit it, even to you—a little envious of Mallory and Brad. I love them, but sometimes…" She couldn't quite utter the truth about the explosion of guilt, jealousy, and anger that sometimes colored her view of the couple, the kindest people on the planet. Sometimes, she hated herself for the way she felt, despite the fact she'd made the choice. She still fought envy, even though Mallory briefed her on parenting decisions and, occasionally, sought her opinions.

"You won't believe what happened at the youth group." Jayne gripped her mug but couldn't quite steady the hot beverage inside. She paused and studied the expression on Tasha's wide, open face. Inner peace radiated from her kind, dark eyes.

In the background, yellow walls peeked out from behind a collage of framed dog photos, illustrating the shelter's countless success stories. Whenever Jayne paused to admire the dogs and review the captions, she clutched a tissue, ready to mop her eyes and cheeks. She couldn't bear to think of mistreated animals, and the rest of the dedicated workers and volunteers felt the same. They worked tirelessly to restore dogs to good health and settle them in suitable homes.

"Do tell." Tasha set down a cinnamon bun and rolled her chair closer.

"Brad organized a games night, so I didn't get a chance to talk much with the kids. If we'd had the regular discussion time, I probably would have avoided trouble." Smirking, Jayne cradled her mug.

"Don't keep me in suspense." Tasha wheeled backward, bit into the bun, and chomped.

Jayne loved lively Tasha, always ready to listen and cheer. "The new doctor in town, Evan Scott, joined us because Brad invited him to volunteer. I went to high school with Evan, but that saga can wait."

"He's single, and you're in love?" Tasha widened her eyes.

"No way." Jayne huffed. Someday, she'd confide in Tasha about their past, but not now. "So…"

"You're driii-ving me crazy, girl." Tasha spun her swivel chair in a full circle and planted her feet to stop the motion.

"We played dodgeball on opposite teams." Smothering a giggle, Jayne leaned forward and recounted the whole incident.

"Nice work, girl." Tasha laughed so hard her cheeks and shoulders shook. "You better do something nice for the poor guy."

Interrupting the gossip session, the phone rang.

"Good morning, Adopt-a-Dog. This is Jayne. How may I help you?" She switched to her professional tone and braced herself for a sad story. Unfortunately, the center kept all too busy for a small town like Prairieville and the surrounding area. Too many people and dogs needed help. Her work mattered and brought fulfillment, but sometimes, it made her heart ache.

"Good morning, Jayne. This is Alice at the doctors' office. Just a reminder about your tetanus shot today at two."

Jayne's mouth dried. Today of all days? She'd forgotten all about her appointment and, definitely, preferred to avoid Evan for as long as possible. Alice was a former school teacher, and she used a friendly but firm tone to manage patients. No messing with Alice. "Oh, I totally forgot…" Could Jayne come up with a good reason to postpone? Working with dogs always held a risk of a bite, so she needed to keep current on tetanus shots. She ticked off reasons in her head, but none sounded plausible. Prairieville Medical Clinic was located just around the corner, so Alice might spot her walking by and wonder about the imaginary excuse.

"I'm sure you know our office policy requires a charge for appointments canceled on short notice, except in emergency situations, of course."

"Uh, sure. I'll see you later." Jayne pictured Alice's precise, gray hairstyle and narrowed eyes. She glanced over at Tasha, shook her head, and crinkled her nose.

"Oh, and one more thing," Alice continued, "Dr. Lewis wants to shift some of his patients—if it's okay with you, of course—over to Dr. Scott."

"No, thank you. That change wouldn't work." Jayne sputtered her horrified reaction. "I'd like to stay with Brad—Dr. Lewis. He knows me. Would you like me to come another day instead?"

"I understand, Jayne." Alice paused. "I'll leave your appointment as scheduled. Two o'clock with Dr. Lewis. We'll see you then."

Jayne waited until she heard Alice end the call,

then clunked down the phone with slightly more force than necessary. "Great. As if a shot isn't bad enough, I'll probably see Evan—Dr. Scott—while I'm there."

"You go, girl." Tasha chuckled and devoured the last of the cinnamon bun, washing it down with a slurp of coffee.

"I feel bad about his glasses, but I don't feel too kindly toward him because of...oh, never mind." Memories stirred in her stomach.

"Wait a minute, girl. You can't drop a teaser and expect me to leave it alone." Tasha thumped a fist on her desk and stared.

"Just something from the past. Ancient history." She swallowed. No need to share her simmering distrust of the guy. "The main issue now is the property situation. He represents the enemy side."

"Competitor maybe, but *enemy* is a little extreme." Tasha glanced at her computer screen and clicked her mouse.

"We owe it to the dogs to acquire that land." In a series of jerky motions, Jayne checked the calendar on her computer, organized the papers on her desk, and practically leapt out of her chair. "I'll leave Sally here with you and go pet dogs for a while." The furry menagerie in the back needed all the love and attention they could get, and she made sure they received the care they deserved, just like children. Tears welled at the image of scruffy, starving, and beaten puppies. In a way, they became her babies, depending on her protection. They filled a gap where a child should reside.

Calmer and focused after thirty minutes with the dogs, Jayne exited the kennel and play area. She brushed hair from her jeans and sweater and washed her hands at the sink in the coffee station. Then she slid into her chair and leaned sideways to pet Sally.

Sally batted the desk with her tail.

"Is your speech ready for the town council tonight?" Tasha spun away from her desk.

"Almost. It's today's project." Jayne had been preparing for tonight's meeting for weeks. The future of Adopt-a-Dog depended on the outcome, and she was determined to get the necessary approvals to proceed with her expansion plan.

"Hey, take a look. What do you think?" Tasha motioned Jayne toward the computer screen. Tasha enlarged a graphic design of an expanded indoor and outdoor exercise area for dogs.

The image illustrated a bright, open area for viewings and playtime and an enlarged, fenced and grassed yard where the dogs could roam freely and safely. It stretched straight behind the existing facility to fill an unused parcel of land that intersected with the rear of the medical clinic.

"Your design is perfect, Tash." Jayne flashed a thumbs-up. "I don't know how the council could refuse. If we get approval for our plan, we'll have the happiest dogs in the province, maybe even in all of Canada." Anticipation and apprehension twisted in her middle. She'd made a huge mistake in her personal life, but she wouldn't botch this project. She'd fight to make life better for dogs.

"Well, I might not go quite that far...but you have vision, girl." Tasha rolled closer to the screen and squinted. "I'll print and mount the design, and you can show the council exactly what you propose."

"Thanks, Tash." Jayne returned to her desk and pushed up her sweater sleeves. She'd make sure her presentation covered all the details and contained facts and answers to address any objections that might arise. "We're so lucky the donation from Mr. Donaldson's estate will cover all the costs."

"I'll answer the phones, and you concentrate without any interruptions." Tasha jumped up and refilled their coffee mugs. She paused for a moment, hands on her ample hips, and surveyed the office.

"Thank you. You're the best." Tasha had a way of knowing whatever Jayne needed and when to leave her alone. Absorbed in her project, Jayne worked right through lunch.

"Time to go to your appointment." Tasha glanced up from her screen and grinned. "Say hello to your friend Dr. Scott for me."

"Not if I can help it." Jayne covered a smile and, on her way out, banged the door.

****

Earlier today, Evan had passed Jayne in the clinic's waiting room. Chairs lined the large window opposite Alice's reception desk. The arrangement was plain and serviceable, but he already pictured updated surroundings.

Jayne perched on the end chair, clutching a magazine with one hand and petting Dudley with the other. She widened her eyes.

Her pale complexion deepened to the same shade of pink as her lips.

Jayne blinked. "You got new glasses." With a piercing gaze, she traced the rim of his frames. "How much do I owe you? I mean it."

"They're not new, but they work." He dropped his hands into his pockets. "No way will I let you pay. Unless you want to settle up with a home-cooked meal. I would never refuse food." Over his leopard-print lab coat, he patted his stomach.

"Uh…you might find cash a safer choice." Jayne raised her eyebrows and half laughed but kept her top lip stretched over her teeth.

"I'm a risk taker. I'll hold out for food." He laughed and had adjusted his glasses higher on his nose. "Serves me right for turning my back on a sharpshooter like you. But I needed new glasses anyway, so I won't hold a grudge."

After the exchange with Jayne, Evan steadied a hand on his stethoscope and ducked into an examination room. In between patients, he pictured Jayne's narrow face. Somewhat serious, with hazel eyes, clear skin, and a faint glow, she might not stand out in a crowd, but she intrigued him all the same. Her eyes shone bright and curious, and her gaze held steady. She left him with the unmistakeable impression of being a person of integrity and someone he'd find honest and soothing. As a teenager, she was a means to a goal. Their connection did not end well. But now, she grabbed his attention for all the right reasons. Still, a vague uneasiness circled like a fly inside his chest.

Late in the afternoon, Brad tossed his lab coat into the laundry bin and led Evan beyond the examination area to his office. "I need to brief you on expansion plans before the council meeting this evening." Brad spread a blueprint on his desk.

With an expanded range of medical and dental services, the clinic could serve a wider radius of the rural area surrounding Prairieville. Any way Evan scrutinized the opportunity, it was win-win-win—good for the medical practice, good for patients, and good for the community. Evan examined the plan. "Makes total sense. I like it."

Brad stubbed a finger onto the diagram. "If we remove the back wall, we can reconfigure the office and build another examination room. On the north side, we'll make space for a physiotherapy center and a dentist. He traced a finger up and down the right side of the diagram.

Evan straightened and rolled his shoulders. "What do you need from me at the council meeting?"

"Support. Your presence will show we're serious and committed." Brad crinkled his eyes. "I'll handle the presentation tonight. When we get the green light, you'll take over and lead the whole project. One more thing. Someone else is competing for the land." He snapped off the lights.

"Oh? I understood the council intended to rubber-stamp our proposal."

"We can't count on a slam dunk. Adopt-a-Dog wants to use the same space."

"By Adopt-a-Dog, you mean Jayne?" Evan dropped his jaw and backed away from the desk. Did that make him her adversary? A clash would definitely not help his cause in advancing their friendship...and possibly more.

"Yep." Brad nodded. "If we're all reasonable adults, we can accept the best proposal will win."

Evan's stomach rumbled, partly from hunger and partly with an uneasy sensation that trouble lay ahead. "Time to go. Dudley." He tapped the side of his leg.

Dudley strolled from the waiting room to join him.

An hour later, leaving Dudley snoozing at home, Evan inhaled a deep breath and prepared for his introduction to the Prairieville Town Council. When he entered the old, stone building, he sniffed a mixture of cool outside air swirled with old wood and floor polish. The first person he spotted was Jayne. Through the crowd milling in the hallway, he recognized the back of her straight hair and her thin figure. She was so slight that if he hugged her tight, he might crush her. But why daydream about an unlikely possibility? He'd already experienced plenty of rejection from important women in his life. What made Jayne any different?

He unzipped his jacket and straightened his shirt. Breathing a little quicker, he sped his footsteps, then dropped back. Why chase Jayne through a crowded hallway? Ahead of him, she zigzagged and disappeared into a doorway on the right. Serious business loomed, and he wouldn't interrupt. Later, could he convince her to socialize with the new doctor in town?

Chapter 4

Jayne sat straight in a wooden chair and clutched her notes. The future of Adopt-a-Dog rode on this meeting. The room buzzed with conversation. A strong turnout of local residents filled seats in a semi-circle lining the perimeter.

The eight-person council sank into leather chairs behind a curved table at the front with wooden wall panelling as a backdrop.

Jayne lowered her gaze and stared at her feet. Her brown, polished boots sprouted like tree stumps above the forest-green carpet. The faint, piney smell of cleaner wafted upward. Heart hammering, she reviewed her key points and visualized herself projecting firm confidence. If she didn't care so much about the dogs that needed a better quality of life, she would never put herself in this public position.

"Let's get started." The mayor, Tommy Calvin, called the meeting to order.

Wearing a neighborly grin and a slightly rumpled, plaid shirt, he belonged in a coffee shop more than in Town Hall, but he was popular, especially with older folks.

"No time like the present." He paused and glanced around the room. "If you brought a present, I've got the time." He threw back his bald head and chortled.

Waiting for the crowd to settle, Jayne slid her gaze

around the room to see who else was there. Maybe if she ignored her hyperactive heart, it would get bored and calm itself before it ejected from her chest. In a town the size of Prairieville, she recognized most of the residents, and a wide cross-section attended tonight. Scanning left, she locked her gaze on a man who stared back.

Evan raised his palm in a scant wave.

The realization jolted her like strong coffee, but she pretended she didn't notice. She rolled her lips inward and gripped her notes so tightly she wrinkled the edges. Evan's presence in town and here at the meeting demonstrated clear evidence that he played a key role in expansion plans.

Weeks ago, Jayne had declared a truce with Brad on the future of the vacant lot backing both Adopt-a-Dog and the medical clinic. She refused to allow business to ruin her relationship with her beloved daughter's adoptive father. Maybe council members would agree his income as a doctor gave him far greater wherewithal to choose a new location than a dog rescue service operating on a shoestring. The decision rested with the town council to determine who would expand onto the coveted property.

Now, in the council chamber, Jayne shivered inside her flannel shirt and adjusted her jacket higher over her shoulders. She rolled her feet to the toes and back to still her shaking knees. Led by Brad and Evan, the medical services supporters were a powerful group. They included other healthcare workers and a handful of residents with special needs. Who could knock a facility that would expand services to families and seniors?

All she could do was appeal to the council's decency to consider the plight of abandoned and mistreated dogs. They couldn't speak for themselves, so she was their voice. Scanning the room, she recognized a few major donors and volunteers for the cause and whooshed out a deep sigh. Maybe their presence and questions would influence the decision.

Just as the meeting began, Tasha rushed into the vacant seat next to Jayne. Breathing heavily, she whispered, "Sorry I'm late."

"Thanks for coming." Jayne relaxed her grip on her speaking notes. Tasha cared about dogs as much as she did, and her positive energy couldn't help but make a difference.

"Folks, we have two housekeeping items and one major discussion on our agenda this evening, so let's dive right in." Mayor Tommy clapped his hands together and swooped them forward into a diving motion. "No splashing, though." He chuckled and jiggled his fat, ruddy cheeks.

Jayne contained an eye roll at his cornball sense of humor and tapped a foot while the council approved a change of meeting time for the winter months and renewed the snow removal contract for the town. Waiting for Tommy to introduce the next part of the agenda, she mentally rehearsed her speech. It wound through her brain in confusing, knotted threads. When the time came, could she present her speaking points in a neat, logical narrative? Would he call her or Brad first? If she spoke first, she could make an immediate, positive impact, but if she followed Brad, she could leave a strong, lasting impression.

"Now, let's attack the meat of the meeting." Mayor

Tommy grinned and rubbed his hands. "Don't know about you, but I like my steak rare and juicy." He squinted at his agenda. "All right. Back to work before I get hungry. Prairieville has a prime parcel of land up for grabs behind Main Street and Prairie Drive. We'll hear two proposals this evening and then decide which project to approve."

Jayne glanced at Brad.

He flicked his gaze back to Mayor Tommy.

Beside Brad, Evan blinked and adjusted his glasses.

Jayne sipped water and set the bottle by her ankles. The broken pair suited him so much better than these temporary ones.

"Brad, you're up." Tommy pointed a stubby finger across the room.

Jayne's stomach fluttered, and the tangle in her brain bunched tighter. Brad had the first word, and she was forced to wait.

He strode to the podium opposite the council members, cleared his throat, and launched into a concise, well-organized presentation.

He was a tough act to follow. His words bounced in and out of her ears without lingering long enough to let her discern the meaning. Finally, she focused her jumbled thoughts, just in time for Brad's wrap-up.

"With the promise of an expanded facility, I attracted a new doctor to Prairieville. I don't want to lose him." Brad swung an arm toward Evan. "Expanded medical services would make Prairieville a better place for our families. Thank you." He nodded and scanned the crowd.

"Thank you, Brad." Tommy nodded and stroked

his chin. "Well said. My parents would appreciate shorter waits for medical appointments. But hey, don't let me influence the vote. I'm only the mayor." He tipped back in his chair, chuckled, and folded his hands over his round torso. "Questions for Brad?"

Most of the council members shook their heads.

Councilperson Wyatt raised a hand. "If you're not selected as the successful bidder, what's next? Have you considered another location for your expanded clinic?" She brushed a stray, blonde curl off her cheek.

"Not yet." Brad grabbed the edges of the podium and drilled his gaze into Tommy. "I hope I don't need to find another location."

"Any other questions from the gallery?" Mayor Tommy plunked his beefy forearms on the table.

Fay, Jayne's most-devoted volunteer, shot up a hand. "Have you ever cared for an abused dog?" Her furrowed forehead, gray hair, and black sweater sent the message she meant business.

"Uh, no." Brad quirked an eyebrow. "I specialize in people, not animals."

Laughter rippled through the room.

Fay blushed.

"I apologize." Brad bowed his head for an instant. "I didn't mean to minimize the situation. I love animals, too."

"If you'd ever fed a scrawny, starving puppy, you wouldn't joke." Fay glared at Brad.

Jayne examined Brad's reaction. He had the decency to nod and lower his gaze. Sometimes, his impulsive quips offended, even though he meant no ill. He was a devoted dad and respected professional in town.

"Dogs need good care and attention, too." Fay clasped her hands in her lap and stiffened.

"Thank you, Brad." Mayor Tommy scanned the room. "Jayne. Where are you? You're next." He swivelled his chair until he spotted her.

Brad nodded and returned to his seat.

"Go get 'em, girl." Tasha bumped her shoulder. "You got this."

Jayne slid off her jacket and, gripping her speaking notes, strode toward the podium. A hush draped the room.

The gallery traced her path.

She felt the burn of Evan's gaze on her profile.

He leaned forward and propped his forearms on his thighs.

A nervous flutter rippled through her stomach. "Good evening, council members, ladies, and gentlemen. Thank you for this chance to speak." Jayne drew in a deep breath, cleared her throat, and glanced over both shoulders. "Thank you to everyone who came to support Adopt-a-Dog. I will share a disturbing story."

****

His gaze glued on Jayne, Evan concentrated on every word Jayne delivered. At first glance, she appeared tiny and timid, but her quiet voice held unmistakeable power. The firm set of her jaw shouted she had overcome adversity and hid more strength than she showed. He wouldn't want to cross her, but he *did* want to cross the room and surround her in a bear hug.

"Please, look at these pictures." She clicked the keyboard on a waiting laptop to reveal a slide projected on a screen to her right.

The room fell so silent the only sound was the whirr of the heating system.

"Last April, a man in a pickup truck stopped in front of Adopt-a-Dog and dropped off a black-and-white dog and her litter of six puppies. The dog had nearly died giving birth, and she was so thin her ribs showed. The man couldn't afford vet bills and didn't know where to turn for help, so he dumped the whole mess on our organization." Jayne paused and fixed her gaze on each member of the council.

An uneasy vibration crept up Evan's spine and twitched in his left eye. The picture captured the desperate plight of the mother dog with her scrawny body, drooping head, and ravenous puppies nuzzling for milk. If his and Brad's proposal won, Adopt-a-Dog would lose. The image of Dudley's lovable face and sturdy body flashed to mind. No animal deserved to be mistreated, and every pet needed a safe home that met its basic needs.

"Already, dogs packed every available spot in the center. My heart broke because I could offer absolutely no space for another dog, especially not an emaciated mother and a litter of hungry puppies." Blinking away moisture, Jayne swallowed and directed a pointed gaze at council members. "I refused to resort to euthanasia. Our philosophy at the shelter gives dogs good and humane lives. They shouldn't die because of thoughtless, human choices."

At the sound of a muffled sniff, Evan tore his gaze from Jayne and glanced over.

A young woman down the row dabbed her eyes with a tissue.

He felt Jayne again snatch his attention like Dudley

grabbed a bone. Her story would touch any animal owner at the meeting. Nobody who loved dogs could ignore the message.

"I had no choice. I packed up the whole bunch and made a temporary home in my basement. My entire place smelled like a kennel."

A murmur of quiet amusement floated over the room.

Jayne paused, and for an instant, she flickered up the corners of her mouth.

Her smiles were sparing at the best of times, and the task at hand must feel very stressful. She was the opponent in the room, but he couldn't help rooting for the cause she represented. She spoke for beings that couldn't speak for themselves.

"But I didn't care." Jayne shook her head, flipped a page of her notes, and switched to another slide. "After a few weeks, I found good homes for the mother and all the pups, so the story ends well."

Evan glanced from Jayne to the image of a transformed dog with a filled-out body, perky ears, and wagging tail. Next to it, a grinning boy cuddled a puppy.

"The overcrowding situation hasn't changed." She forced both palms onto the podium in a single drumbeat.

Evan straightened, rubbed his thighs, and waited for her final pitch. He couldn't judge how the council would react, but she better finish strong. Both causes showed merit. Both were well organized and professionally presented. But they appealed to different interests and priorities, so the decision might prove difficult.

Jayne clicked to another picture, showing rows of kennels and a small exercise and play area. "If you approve our expansion plan, you will allow us to enlarge the exercise area and to free space to accommodate more dogs. You'll address a real need in our community. Thank you for considering this proposal."

"Thank you, Jayne." Mayor Tommy spun his chair in a full rotation. "Whew. If all that information didn't make me dizzy, that ride just did. Questions, anyone?"

"Do you have the funding to expand?" Councilperson Robertson furrowed his forehead and rubbed a temple.

"Yes." Jayne nodded and clutched her notes. "In the last year, we received a government grant and an endowment from a local resident's estate. Now we just need the space."

"Other questions?" Tommy tapped a pen on the table.

"Have you considered a move to the edge of town?" Peter White pointed an arthritic finger to the west.

"Not at this point." Jayne swept her gaze across the panel and over both shoulders. "We can afford a renovation in our current location but not the cost of relocating and building new."

Evan bounced his attention around the room and back to Jayne. She delivered answers in a firm, confident tone. No one could doubt her dedication to animals and commitment to the project. He inhaled a deep breath but couldn't dissolve the vague tension in his chest. Why was he so sympathetic to the opposing bid?

"Time's up." Tommy slammed a palm onto the table. "Normally, the council would recess and then vote. I don't know about the rest of this motley crew, but I could use more than a few minutes to consider these proposals." He straightened and swivelled from side to side. "We'll reconvene in two weeks and decide. Now, go home, everybody, and cheer for the Prairie Winters."

Evan crinkled his forehead. Had he heard right? Did the mayor just cut short a meeting to watch a professional hockey game on TV?

Jayne arched her eyebrows and darted to retrieve her jacket from where it stretched over the back of her chair.

Judging by her stiff body language, she did not appreciate the abrupt end to the meeting, and neither did Evan. He rose and zipped his jacket. "Guess we wait." He faced Brad and shrugged.

"I can't believe the way that guy operates." Huffing, Brad shook his head. "With all due respect to Jayne, I figured our proposal would win."

"She did a good job. I'll stick around to congratulate her." Evan waved Brad forward. "See you tomorrow."

With sharp gestures, Jayne launched into an animated conversation with the frizzy-haired woman beside her.

The woman hugged her and, next to Jayne, inched toward the door.

Could he catch Jayne alone? Evan loitered, bent, and retied a shoelace. Jayne's companion remained glued to her side. Impatience urged him to interrupt. In long strides, he joined the pair. "Good job, Jayne."

Jayne jerked her head toward him and glowered. "Thanks, but you can't mean it."

Her comment stung. She might as well have slapped his cheek. If he couldn't offer a sincere compliment, he wouldn't have said anything. "I do." He matched her slower pace. "You delivered a convincing pitch."

"You can't support me. You're the...opposition." Jayne narrowed her eyes and hunched her shoulders.

"Competition maybe, but not an enemy. Have a good evening." He burst ahead without a backward glance. He could take a hint. This evening was the wrong time to get better acquainted with his former classmate. A date might be a bad and unlikely idea, but he couldn't help picturing them together, laughing and holding hands. She just needed more time to be persuaded. Against his better judgment, sooner or later, he'd find a way.

Chapter 5

"You sure told him." Tasha raised her eyebrows and, next to Jayne, hustled outside. "I felt sorry for the poor guy."

Out on the street, Jayne zipped her jacket higher against the chilly breeze. "Yeah, well, I can't stand people saying things that aren't true." Maybe Tasha had a point. Her reaction might have been a little harsh. "I didn't mean to be rude, but I needed to show assertiveness." Guilt flooded her like a prairie rainstorm. She knew well the weight of having done the wrong thing, and she constantly battled it. She still hadn't completely forgiven herself for everything that led to Cara.

"If you hurry, you can still catch him and apologize." Tasha nudged Jayne's elbow. "Go. Right now."

"But…" Jayne shook her head, then stopped. She taught the teenage girls at the youth group to apologize when they made a mistake and to make things right. "Now?" She hesitated for another second. In the crisp outside air, her temper cooled, and her embarrassment heated. Prairieville was a small town. She'd likely run into Evan pretty often, especially if he volunteered with the youth. For her own peace of mind, she couldn't afford to create bad feelings.

"Now." Tasha swung her arm toward Evan, who

gained ground up ahead. "See you tomorrow. You can share all the juicy details."

Jayne's throat dried enough to crack, but before she reconsidered, she accelerated and broke into a jog with her purse swinging from her shoulder. Breathing rapidly, she filled her lungs with the comforting autumn smell of burning firewood and smouldering leaves. Sniffing, she absorbed the smoky air. She pictured a family enjoying an evening campfire in their backyard. They were lucky to share a home and a life within a close circle—very different than hers. Suddenly, the air bit instead of soothed. As she caught up, she slowed and caught her breath. "Evan, wait."

He stopped, rotated, and wrinkled his forehead.

"I need to say something." She took a quick breath.

He quirked an eyebrow and slid a slow smile across his face.

Instantly, she regretted her decision to follow. She didn't need to be the butt of his amusement. No doubt, he'd recount the incident to Brad and give him reason to tease.

"Okay, sure." He stuffed his hands into his jacket pockets. "What's up?"

"I, uh…" She glanced at her boots and then at his scuffed runners. He might be a big-time doctor now, but he remained the same guy from high school, who mortified her more than once. Irritation prickled her throat. Did she really need to apologize? "I'm sorry for…" Remorse tripped up her words. "Uh, for snapping after the meeting. I just care so much about those poor dogs crammed together." Her words covered part of the truth. She couldn't apologize for holding a grudge. Evan deserved her long-held resentment.

"Thanks, but no problem. I'll survive." Grinning, he shrugged and shifted from foot to foot.

"Okay, good." Shivering in the wind, Jayne glanced in the direction of her house. "Well, I better run."

Evan stayed planted. "If you want to compensate, you could join me for coffee." He chuckled and nodded his head in the direction of Sam's.

"Pardon?" She wanted to get home to Sally and take her for an evening walk. She'd said she was sorry. Her guilt was already dissolving like a bath bomb. But now, he expected more. She stretched to her full height and stiffened. He showed a lot of nerve, just like the kid all those years ago in English class. She paused. Should she agree?

A pickup truck rumbled by and interrupted the peaceful hush of Main Street. Behind Evan, a soft glow lit racks of tools, screws, and wire visible through the hardware store window. She belonged here in Prairieville. Life felt simpler than in Regina, where big mistakes happened in a heartbeat.

"A coffee break. It won't take much time." Closing his lips over his grin, he tugged his hands out of his pockets.

"Sorry, in the evening, I avoid caffeine." She half faced him and shook her head. Her knees quivered. He knew how to burrow under her skin—and not in a good way.

"No problem. How about herbal tea or hot chocolate or water…or nothing at all?" He shifted and grinned again. "Just humor me. Keep me company while I scarf down a sandwich."

Did she want to accompany him to Sam's? The

popular restaurant was the town hub, and the place hummed most of the day and evening. She'd bump into people she knew, and tomorrow, word would spread that she and Evan were an item. A simple apology could accelerate into a full-blown rumor as quickly as rabbits multiplied in Prairieville. No, thanks.

"C'mon." He waved her across the street in the direction of the café. "Don't tell me you can refuse chocolate cake or peanut butter cookies."

She needed to politely decline. She might be a touch hungry, but she could throw together a snack at home. Besides, Sally waited, probably scanning out the front window. She opened her mouth to say no, but something short-circuited in her brain. "I guess so." She released the brakes, and a load of uncertainty sped down a hill right into the pit of her stomach. "But I can't stay long."

What had she done? Now, she had to make conversation with a guy she didn't even like. He'd probably ask her about her life since high school and what enticed her back to Prairieville. The edited version of her past raced through her mind. She didn't need to share details she preferred to conceal. They were none of his business. Of course, in a small town, he'd hear soon enough, and then he probably wouldn't act so eager to spend time together.

"Let's go." He stepped off the curb.

For an instant, she hesitated. "Okay." She matched his pace, but couldn't think of anything clever to say. Maybe she'd treat herself to a dessert.

Sam, owner of his namesake diner, had won a provincial baking contest, and his skill showed.

At least, she'd enjoy something about the visit. But

seriously, why did she agree? Would Evan count a quick coffee break as a first date?

****

Inside the café, country music, clattering dishes, and murmured conversation swirled around the delicious aroma of apple pie. "I'll treat." Maneuvering ahead, Evan headed to the counter, positioned to one side, next to a display case of desserts and in front of an opening to the kitchen. "Just to show I hold no hard feelings. What'll you have?" He wouldn't give Jayne time to change her mind. The way she glanced at the door and covered her mouth with her fingertips, she might bolt any second. He perused the menu board of specials mounted on a wall behind the counter and landed on a roasted chicken sandwich and coleslaw.

"No, I'll buy." She elbowed her way beside him. "If you won't let me pay for your new glasses, the least I can do is cover a snack."

"Snack? I want a late dinner." He patted his stomach. "Gotta keep up my weight." He could stand to lose a few pounds, but he wasn't too concerned. His shoulders, arms, and legs were still firm and muscular. He could still counsel patients on the benefits of a healthy lifestyle. "Nope, I insist. You can pay the next time." If she owed him, then maybe she'd agree to join him again.

She huffed and clicked her tongue. "I won't argue." She stared at the menu board and, finally, settled on orange-spice tea and a butterscotch square.

She could afford the calories. Unlike him, she might need to tie herself to a post so she didn't blow away on a windy day.

"Hey, Jayne. I'll deliver it to the table." A grinning,

fortyish guy wearing a hairnet called through the window to the kitchen.

"Great. Thanks, Sam." She wove through the tables and greeted several people.

Evan settled in a booth near the window.

She chatted and, a couple of times, tipped her head in his direction. People probably wondered about the newcomer, even though he wasn't a true stranger. Still, fifteen years had rolled by since he called Prairieville home. Some people might remember he snagged the top scholarship at Prairieville High, but the way he achieved top marks wouldn't impress anybody.

While he waited for the food and Jayne, he scanned the café. The place was casual and cozy, surrounding him with warm earth tones and sepia-colored photos of prairie scenes and local wildlife. He might as well be plunked right in the middle of a wheat field. Wooden flooring and worn booths added to the rustic décor. He recognized a few faces from this evening's meeting and a few from the past. The elderly, wrinkled woman seated in one corner had taught history.

He let his gaze trail Jayne's zigzag path until she arrived at the booth. "I take it he's the owner?" Evan nodded toward the kitchen.

Nodding, she slid onto the brown, padded seat opposite him. "He graduated a few years before us. He left for chef school and then returned. His café took off right away."

"I gather you know everybody in town." For now, he'd steer the topic away from the town council meeting. He grabbed a bundle of cutlery wrapped in a gold napkin and spun it on the table. How long would he live here before he belonged? He had chased the university scholarship that led to medical school, but he was a prairie boy at heart and never felt at home in Ontario.

"Just about." She leaned on an elbow, rested her chin on a hand, and tapped fingers against her lips.

"Must be nice." He relocated to Prairieville for the job, but more than anything, he craved a cozy, familiar community. The opportunity here wouldn't appeal to everyone, but it suited him for a fresh start.

"Most of the time." Propping her forearms on the table, she clasped her hands. "Sometimes, I feel a bit under a microscope. My parents live in town, too, so they know everything. Not that I do anything shocking, but still, I don't always enjoy privacy."

"I see your point." He'd never dealt with hovering parents. Dad passed away several years ago, and Mom remarried and moved to Victoria, British Columbia. Left alone, he didn't even consider moving close. She enjoyed her own life with a new husband and grown stepchildren, and he wouldn't intrude into their tight circle. His chest throbbed around the empty spot where family should reside.

Unrolling the napkin around his cutlery, he peeked over and around her hands. She must feel terribly self-conscious about her teeth. They were far from magazine perfect, but hiding them only drew more attention. He wouldn't broach the topic now, but maybe if he grew closer, he'd let her know. Her teeth made her unique and not less attractive.

"Here you go." Balancing food and beverages on a tray, Sam arrived at their table. Tall and thin with brown, scrambled hair jammed under his hairnet, he bent and served their food with a flourish.

Evan inhaled a light scent of garlic.

"I'm Sam. New in town?" He lowered the tray to one side.

"Evan Scott." He stuck out his right hand. "Not Scott Evans. With two first names, I hear variations."

"Thanks for the heads-up." Chuckling, Sam wiped his free hand on his apron. "Now I'll probably call you Scott."

"I grew up here and just moved back." Evan eyed his plate. The thick sandwich, garnished with a dill pickle, made his mouth water. "Jayne and I went to high school together. She was thrilled to see me."

Jayne rolled her eyes. "Overjoyed."

Her voice dripped with sarcasm, but he'd take it as a joke. She'd already apologized once this evening, so she likely didn't mean to jab him again. Or did she?

"She's nicer than she sounds. Right, Jayne?" Sam squeezed her shoulder.

"Possibly." With her lips together, she barely smiled.

"Can I get you anything else?" Sam scanned the table. "No? Enjoy your food." He hustled back to the kitchen.

Evan chomped a large mouthful. A rich combination of spicy meat, tangy sauce, and fresh tomatoes satisfied his craving for comfort food.

Without a word, Jayne sipped her tea and sampled the butterscotch square.

He swallowed and used a napkin to wipe a drip off his chin. Should he dare raise their competition? He lifted the sandwich, paused to gather the right words, and set it back on the plate. "Your presentation stirred people. Council needs to wrestle with a tough decision."

Jayne clunked her mug and sloshed tea onto the table. "If I'd known you'd raise that topic again, I wouldn't have joined you."

"Sure." He stuffed another large bite into his mouth. He'd hate to agitate her and send her running like Bethany. The recurring sense of failure draped over his shoulders like a cold blanket. In just a few years, his ex-wife's loving expression had chilled to an indifferent stare. "What do you want to talk about?"

She shrugged, took a bite of the square, and licked her top lip.

Guitar twangs accompanying a mellow voice filled the air and covered the gap in their conversation. He didn't mind the folksy sound. It surrounded and, in a way, comforted. The music reminded him Prairieville was home, and no one could ever steal his roots. "Might as well pick up where we left off. What have you done for the last fifteen years?" He chewed and gave her time to think. She likely wouldn't jump to answer.

She opened and closed her mouth. Again, she shrugged. "Not much, really."

"I don't believe you." Nobody lived a life in limbo. She was probably just too modest to share. He examined her narrow cheeks. If the flush deepened any more, it would rival the color of the ketchup bottle clustered with the salt and pepper at the edge of the table.

"Nothing very interesting, anyway." She popped the last bite of her treat into her mouth and lowered her gaze to the empty plate.

"Why don't you tell me about the uninteresting things?" He shifted his gaze from her face to the window, reflecting the bustling diner superimposed on the starry night outside.

"I went to University of Regina." She glanced at his sandwich. "At first, I wanted to be a vet. But by the time I finished my science degree, I was tired of school. Then, the cost of vet college…" She shook her head and furrowed her forehead.

A sharp memory sliced his concentration. Back in high school, they vied for the top scholarship, but he scooped it. His high English mark had helped, and she made it possible. Thanks to the financial assistance he received, he had never shared her worries about the cost of schooling. A fist of guilt nudged his stomach.

"After I graduated, I managed a chain of pet stores and volunteered at an animal shelter. Then I moved back to Prairieville." She twisted her napkin.

"Now, you run Adopt-a-Dog and volunteer with the youth group." Her past sounded pretty average. She likely wouldn't feel comfortable at all with the black marks he left in Toronto. A broken marriage and a bitter heart probably didn't rank on her list of desirable characteristics. "Did the job lure you?" Something must have changed to prompt her to leave the city. He speared a forkful of coleslaw and waited. Getting her to share was like squeezing the last bit of toothpaste out of the tube.

"Connections with family and friends." She clutched her mug with both hands. "I wanted to live closer to the people I love. The job worked out well, too." She paused, blinked several times, and lifted the mug to her lips.

She spoke so quietly he barely heard, but her underlying message was clear. She had suffered and worked hard to recover. "Have you always been single?" The moment he asked, he could have stuffed a fist into his mouth. His question was innocent enough, but he didn't want to pry. She sent strong vibes she valued privacy. Now she'd probably skitter away like a startled deer.

She widened her eyes and studied her tea.

Was she even going to answer? He shifted slightly forward and followed her gaze.

"I've never been married." She clutched the cup, and the liquid vibrated inside.

"Oh. I'm divorced." He grimaced and set down his fork. At least, she didn't gasp or raise her eyebrows. He set his napkin beside his plate. The light meal satisfied, and her company beat eating alone at home. At this point, he didn't need to spill everything about his past. She'd probably never guess the bitterness that simmered beneath his jovial exterior. Bethany wasn't the first woman who'd rejected him. The pattern started early with his birth mother.

"Time to leave." She checked her watch. "Sally needs her nightly walk." She grabbed her jacket and stood.

Jayne didn't press for any details on his background. Maybe she'd ask more questions another time—*if* she agreed to another get-together. "Dudley charms the ladies. Sometime, we should team up for a walk." Evan slid out of the booth.

"I know." Jayne flew a hand to her mouth and laughed. "Dudley cozied up to Sally at the youth group. Of course, she never met another golden retriever she didn't like."

Maybe Jayne would consent to meet him again for

her dog's sake. She acted a little stiff and aloof, but she relaxed when she talked about Sally. Her natural reserve was a little mysterious, like a package he wanted to unwrap. He liked her company, except for the tension over that coveted parcel of land. He didn't need the most gorgeous woman in town—just a genuine and understanding person. Of course, a sense of humor wouldn't hurt.

"Thanks again for the snack." At the door, she raised a hand in a half wave. "See you around."

"Hope so." If he was lucky, he'd run into her sooner rather than later. For an hour, his loneliness had dissolved in the warm, country atmosphere. But why kid himself? A woman would stir up his insecurities, and he didn't need the uncertainty.

"Maybe Friday at the youth group," she called over her shoulder.

"You meet again Friday?" He rubbed his neck. Suddenly, he felt too warm. Did Jayne just invite him to the gathering? Was she only being polite? Or did she want to spend more time together like he craved?

Chapter 6

"You have no idea what you forced me into last evening." The next morning, at Adopt-a-Dog, Jayne poured coffee and grimaced at Tasha. "Thanks a lot, girlfriend." She inhaled the rich aroma mixed with the scent of animal fur and dry kibble, a combination only a dog and coffee lover could appreciate but warmed Jayne's heart every single workday.

Assorted yips and woofs from the kennel area punctuated their conversation.

"What? I only suggested you do the right thing and apologize." Laughing, Tasha stirred her coffee. Still grinning, she headed to her desk. "Do tell."

Jayne recounted the details. Avoiding Tasha's intense gaze, Jayne studied her friend's burgundy sweater and paisley headband.

"You are a sweet, smart cookie, girl. A cutie, too, in a conservative way." Tasha stretched taller. "Hey, there he is."

Did conservative mean boring? Jayne glanced down at her old blue jeans and beige sweater, then tilted up her chin and squinted to get a better view out the front window.

Evan and Dudley paced by on their way to work.

"Wave, Jayne." Tasha popped closer to the window, grinned, and waved but couldn't catch Evan's attention.

Jayne crossed her arms. "I'm not interested." A funny sensation rose and fell in her stomach. He *was* attractive and fun. "Looks like *he* is. What are you afraid of, anyway?" Tasha tapped Jayne's shoulder.

"Nothing. I'm not scared." Jayne took a deep breath. "But the strangest thing happened."

"Ooh, sounds interesting." Never drifting her gaze off Jayne, Tasha scooted back to her chair.

Jayne gripped her coffee mug. Evan was a mature professional, but every time she searched his large eyes and wide smile, she remembered inconsiderate, teenage Evan. Worse, she imagined his raised eyebrows at the situation with Cara. "To my total surprise, I invited him to the youth group on Friday, almost like I wanted him to come."

"Surprises are good, girl." Tasha stared and blinked three times before she spun her chair toward her desk. "You need a little excitement in your life."

"Whatever you say." Jayne rolled her eyes.

At that moment, her office phone rang.

She welcomed the timely interruption. "Good morning. Adopt-a-Dog. How can I help you?" She'd dive into work and forget her social life. She needed to strategize and build extra support in the next two weeks, or she'd never achieve her goal of expansion.

"Good morning." A male voice rumbled a greeting.

He emphasized both words and delivered them with a tone of familiarity like she should recognize his voice. Of course, she did, but she paused and waited for him to continue.

"Jayne, it's Evan."

Why did he call her at work? What did he need? Her heart beat much faster than normal. She rotated, so

Tasha couldn't see her wide-eyed expression.

"I won't interrupt long."

Jayne contained a huff. She didn't have time to chat. Office talk with Tasha didn't count. She petted Sally with her free hand in a motion meant to soothe herself but didn't.

"Do you and Sally have lunch plans? Because Dudley and I would like to invite you on a walk and a picnic."

"Uh…" She had not expected to see Evan until Friday at the youth group. Last evening, she consented to snacks as a one-time occasion because she felt guilty for her brush-off. Now, he proposed a lunch date? If she declined, she'd suffer Tasha's scolding all afternoon. She glanced at Sally.

The dog's tongue lolled sideways out of her mouth, and her tail fanned a spray of dog hair. She'd welcome any adventure, and the extra fresh air wouldn't hurt.

Tasha left her desk, planted herself in front of Jayne, and stared.

She must have a sixth sense that hinted something interesting might happen.

"Say *yes,*" she whispered the words and nodded her head.

"I guess so. At least, Sally would have fun with Dudley." Jayne flushed from her neck to the roots of her hair. "But I didn't pack a lunch."

Tasha grinned and shot two thumbs-up.

Jayne grimaced and flicked a hand like she swatted an annoying fly.

"Don't worry about food. I'll order takeout from Sam's and pick you up at noon. See you then." He clicked off the call before Jayne said goodbye.

"You got yourself a lunch date, girl." Tasha leaped and held up her hand for a high five.

Why did she agree? Did she make a mistake? Uncertainty storming in her chest, she tapped Tasha's palm.

Sally panted and circled.

From the back, even through the closed door, a muffled chorus of barks filled the room.

Did the dogs cheer, too? "Enough." Jayne pretended to glare at Tasha, but she smothered a smile. "I'll pet the pups. Then we'll plan." She headed for the kennels to reset her day to a fresh and familiar start.

The staff and volunteers bustled outside to clean the yard, leaving her alone to give each dog individual attention and a crunchy treat. Next to Cara, dogs brought her some of her biggest joys, and she'd fight for their cause. The new doctor in town would not stand in her way.

She opened the gate to a pen and scratched a scruffy terrier's chin. Usually, when she cared for the dogs, she focused on nothing else, but today, her thoughts zigzagged like a border collie herding sheep.

Lunch with Evan sounded suspiciously like a date. Could she relax and enjoy the time together? Did too many factors lurk in the way? At this point, why add stress? She extended a biscuit to a pug and laughed when he rejected it. Dogs showed preferences like people. Did she prefer time alone to an excursion with Evan?

Straightening, she took a deep breath and continued along the aisle between rows of kennels. Now, her heartrate bounced like she overdosed on caffeine. Inside the next stall, she received a gentle lick on the cheek from a husky mix with one blue eye and one brown eye. Dogs offered unconditional love, just like sweet, little Cara. She filled, yet expanded, a hole in Jayne's heart. But her loss and hurt never fully eased.

So far, Evan gave no indication he knew the truth about Cara. Would he judge Jayne by her mistake? In small towns, news spread like fleas, so he'd probably hear murmurs soon. Rumors could hurt worse than the truth.

"Don't worry. I'll find you a good home." Inside another cage, she thumped the sides of a boisterous chocolate lab. Cute dogs soon found an eager owner. She felt sorry for the homely dogs or those with temperament issues nobody wanted. Every time somebody selected a pet, she screened them as prospective owners. More than once, she had refused an unsuitable match. "Relax, buddy." On her next stop, she rubbed behind a spaniel's ears.

Slowing her pace, she inhaled the familiar, musky aroma until her lungs might burst. Farther along the walkway, she paused and soothed a shaking, ragamuffin dog with an extra reassuring pat. How long until lunchtime? Could she change her mind? Would that nervous twinge in her middle even allow her to eat? Thirty minutes later, and just as muddled, Jayne barged into the office area. Answering routine inquiries and ordering supplies, she pounded her computer keyboard.

"Here's what I propose, girl." Tasha held up a scribbled list.

As usual, she burst with enthusiasm. Jayne loved her loyal friend and dedicated employee.

"Let's ask everybody on our contact list to lobby different council members." On her fingers, Tasha checked off her first idea.

"I agree." The more ownership Tasha felt, the more energy she'd devote.

"You appeal to Brad and Evan to scout a new location." Tasha ticked another finger.

"Ugh." Jayne wrinkled her nose. The task was her responsibility, but she didn't welcome it one bit, especially because she couldn't jeopardize her relationship with Brad and Mallory. With Evan, she had nothing to lose. Or did she? A shiver of uncertainty rippled across her shoulders, and she crossed her arms.

"Bet you didn't think of this one." Tasha whacked a third finger.

"Hit me." Jayne raised her eyebrows and adjusted her glasses. Tasha's dramatic pause might mean a brilliant idea. Then again, she specialized in drama, so her suggestion might not be as earth-shattering as she hoped.

"We'll ask for support from all the veterinarians in the area." Tasha held up both palms and wiggled her fingers. "Ready, girl? I just delivered a solid plan."

"Your starburst hands impress me almost as much as your good thinking." Laughing, Jayne imitated Tasha's finger waggle. "All right, let's start. We can't waste time." She propped her elbows on her desk, rested chin on hands, and squeezed her eyes shut. Could the welfare of dogs compete with human healthcare?

"Go comb your hair, girl." Tasha pointed at the clock. "You want to impress your date, don't you?"

Jayne snapped her gaze to Tasha and opened her mouth to disagree, but she clamped it shut. Tasha's laugh shook her whole body, and Jayne wouldn't give her the satisfaction of a strong reaction. "Nope, I don't care." She shrugged, tossed her head, and let her hair land wherever it fell.

"I don't believe you." Tasha quirked an eyebrow. "But do what you want. Why try to look your best for your future boyfriend?"

"Remind me why I call you my best friend." Jayne mock huffed, stretched, and peered out the window. Actually, she didn't mind the banter. Tasha's sense of humor and relentless teasing only showed how much she cared. Tasha turned her back and dug into her lunch bag.

Free of scrutiny, Jayne finger combed her hair and flicked her bangs so they sat in place across her forehead. Maybe Tasha had a point. Not that she wanted to impress Evan, but she didn't need to appear in public with messy hair.

The outside air would feel good—a classic, crisp October day with bright sunshine and a bare hint of wind. Right now, a picnic outing sounded okay, except a ball of anticipation rolled through her middle, bounced, and knocked her appetite out of the way. The day shone ideal, but could the unsettling company possibly match the weather?

****

Evan couldn't miss Adopt-a-Dog. He stopped in front of the eye-catching, white building decorated with painted, black paw prints. A red sign with white lettering stretched across the front and confirmed he was in the right place. From the sidewalk, he peeked through the wide, waist-high window and waved to grab Jayne's attention.

Within seconds, next to Sally, she jostled out the doorway.

"Hey, Sally. Say hi to your date, Dudley." Evan petted both dogs with vigorous swipes.

Jayne paused.

Sally leapt in circles, wagging her tail and sniffing her friend.

Taking stock of Jayne's appearance, Evan sensed his heartbeat quicken. She wore faded blue jeans, brown ankle boots, and a beige, cable-knit sweater topped with a moss-green quilted vest. Her relaxed dress suited a casual workplace and an impromptu picnic. Her eyes gleamed with intelligence, but she frequently lowered her gaze like she needed to protect something inside. But what?

"You planned great weather." Holding Sally's leash, Jayne gained speed.

He chuckled at her quip. "Glad you approve. Our lunch should be ready." Inhaling full breaths of crisp, sweet autumn air, Evan steered Dudley along the sidewalk toward Sam's. His stomach had growled with hunger at the office, but now, as he hustled down Main Street beside Jayne, an odd queasiness took over.

He had arranged this lunch to prove he wouldn't mention the expansion plan every time they met. They might be competitors, but the land issue didn't need to color their whole relationship. They both loved golden retrievers and dogs, in general. Even if a slight cloud lingered from high school, the shadow belonged in the distant past. Now, they were work neighbors. Soon, he might join her as a youth group leader.

Anticipation tapped in his chest. She was attractive in a natural, unassuming way—the exact opposite of Bethany. Smooth as cheesecake on the surface, Jayne had already proven she had a firm base. In between, he had much more to discover. He loved a dessert with layers.

He glanced down at Dudley. The dog's entire body wagged like he smelled a steak dinner.

Every few steps, Dudley nudged Sally.

She nipped and romped until she strained her leash.

Jayne held on tight and practically jogged to keep up with the two, playful pups. "We need a dog park in town." She tugged Sally into line. "Of course, sometimes, owners take chances and allow dogs to run free in the country, but then we risk an encounter with a porcupine or a skunk." She waved a hand in front of her nose. "Sometimes, coyotes roam the fields, too."

"What about the school yard?" Evan breathed a little easier. The small talk perked up his appetite. Lucky thing, considering he ordered the Country Combo for two. Judging by the description of the special, including sandwiches, fries, and cookies, he'd unpack enough food to feed them for supper, too.

"Yeah, but only when school's out."

"If you hold Dudley's leash, I'll dash in and grab our order." Arriving at the cafe, he handed over the leash and left Jayne and the dogs parked in front.

A clamor of clattering dishes and lively conversation greeted him, and the air hung thick with the tantalizing aroma of fresh bread and corn chowder.

"Back already?" Through the window between the kitchen and dining areas, Sam grinned and wiped his forehead with the back of a hand.

"Yep, I could be a new regular." Evan fished in a pocket for his wallet. "My order comes with a preferred-customer discount, right?" He chuckled, and the rest of the tension in his stomach flitted away. He'd soon fit in with the locals and have some fun again.

"You got it. I prefer all my customers, so I charge everybody the same." Sam slid two paper bags onto the ledge for the server to grab. "How do you think I pay for my winter holidays?" Laughing, he adjusted his hair net and gave a partial wave. "Is that Jayne waiting outside with the dogs?" He peered through the restaurant's large front window. "Enjoy."

Outside, Jayne chatted with an ash-blonde, middle-aged woman wearing a purple sweat suit and jiggling a matching water bottle.

Clutching the bags, Evan approached and waited next to Jayne.

She glanced his way and cleared her throat. "Louanne, this is Evan Scott. You might remember him from years ago. He grew up here." She gripped the leashes. "Louanne is Mom's best friend."

"Iris and I met when we were just tykes in elementary school." Louanne scrutinized Evan. "Your name is familiar. You won a big scholarship to some fancy university in Toronto." She raised her voice and tapped a finger on her chin.

"Yeah, I was fortunate." Evan shifted and glanced at Jayne. Did she remember she helped him win?

"Your mom moved to Victoria. You got married and divorced."

He raised his eyebrows. Did she keep up with everybody's life milestones? He nodded, reclaimed Dudley's leash, and sidestepped away.

Louanne shouted facts and waved her hands. The water sloshed inside the bottle, and she darted her gaze up and down Evan and over to Jayne. She widened her eyes.

Louanne reminded him of a game show contestant the way she spilled her excitement. The chance encounter must be the highlight of her day. The downside of small-town life hurtled back, and Evan wanted to duck her commentary.

"Now, you're the new doctor in town." She flicked a finger at his chest.

He nodded. "Very impressive. What's my middle name?" Juggling the bags of food along with Dudley's leash, he smiled and extended a hand.

"Oh, you're too funny." Louanne giggled and crinkled her eyes into a squint.

"Pleased to get reacquainted." Evan shook her hand, then repositioned the bags. "Now, time to eat."

"Have fun, kids." Louanne tootled off in the opposite direction, pumping her arms at a furious pace.

"Whew, what a whirlwind." Chuckling, Evan shook his head. "She supervised the lunch program at school. Nothing slipped by her unnoticed. One day, she called my mom to report I dropped and stepped on my tuna sandwich. She claimed I did it on purpose." He paused. "She might have been right." No doubt, Louanne would broadcast the news of his return, even before the picnic ended.

"Mostly, she has a kind heart, but sometimes, I remind myself to appreciate the whole package." Jayne shrugged and tilted sideways to run a hand down Sally's wriggling body.

Evan stared ahead to the park. Even from a distance, he spotted the vivid orange, gold, and yellow leaves drifting to the ground. The day couldn't get any better—perfect fall weather and the ideal companions for an outing. "Let's sit over there." Jayne gestured to the right, where several mustard-colored benches faced a large play structure. "Sally won't wander." She unhooked the dog's leash. "What about Dudley?"

"Dudley sticks close to food." Evan laughed and felt a warm rush at her twinkling eyes and upturned lips. She must have forgotten about her teeth for a second because the crossed tips peeked out. He plunked the lunch bags between them.

Then she dropped her upper lip back into place and smothered her laughter. "Nice selection." Jayne spread napkins to convert the bench into a makeshift table and unwrapped her food.

"Cheers." He lifted a thick sandwich in an exaggerated toast. "No, Dudley. Go play with Sally."

Dudley rested his saggy chin on Evan's knee and drooled.

"Brad told me about the youth retreat next weekend." Evan glanced at Jayne.

"Oh?" Jayne paused mid chew. She wrinkled her forehead and brushed away a few stray hairs that blew across her lips.

"He's short of male volunteers to chaperone." He dunked a fry into a pool of ketchup, popped it into his mouth, and chewed the salty bite. "He asked me to consider helping."

"What do you think?" She held her sandwich poised for a bite.

"I'm not sure." He munched a pickle seasoned with flavorful dill and studied her expression. Two lines appeared above the bridge of her nose. She wasn't thrilled with the idea.

"Brad's right. Tasha and I will supervise the girls, but he could use some support with the guys." She dabbed her mouth with a napkin. "Some of the kids' dads are volunteer firefighters, so they never leave town at the same time."

She stopped short of encouraging him to join the expedition. Did she doubt he was capable or appropriate because he wasn't a dad or well-known to the kids? Did she dislike his company so much she didn't want to spend more time together? "I said I'd think about it." Evan stuffed the last bite of sandwich into his mouth. "All gone." He clapped his hands to shoo Dudley. "Now, go play." He pointed toward Sally.

Jayne swallowed and dropped her gaze to the cookies.

"I like kids as patients." He'd love to be a parent, too. Too late, he'd learned Bethany cared more about her career than motherhood. He swallowed. "I don't know if I offer the right experience to chaperone."

"Believe in yourself." Jayne gazed directly at Evan's face.

He jerked back. Could she see the tender spot he hid? Did she sense he needed encouragement? Instantly, he felt the sun shine warmer.

Jayne glanced at her watch. "We better pack the leftovers and hurry back to work. Sally, come." She folded a napkin around two cookies and tucked them into a pocket. "Thanks for lunch and the afternoon snack." She curved up the corners of her lips.

Her eyes glinted. Did she enjoy his company? "Come, Dudley." The brief personal connection broken, Evan tossed their garbage like a basketball shot into the nearby receptacle. "Two points for my team." Strolling beside Jayne, he drank in the brilliant light, sniffed the sharp scent of end-of-season flowers, and absorbed the peaceful atmosphere.

He had never expected a friendly lunch to lead to an almost-warm invitation. Attraction tingled up his back and circled his chest. Prairieville promised a new beginning. Did a fresh start include romance?

Chapter 7

Jayne walked the long way home from work, left Sally in the back yard, and flopped on one of the twin, tan loveseats in her compact living room. She rested her head on a red toss cushion and stared out the front window at stark tree branches. All combined, the pressure of drumming up support for the Adopt-a-Dog expansion, avoiding overt tension over the competing proposal, and the lunch conversation with Evan exhausted her.

Her phone rang, and she snatched it out of a pocket, checked Call Display, and considered whether to answer. "Hi, Mom." She mustered a calm and patient tone. Right now, she was not in the mood for a chat. She had hoped her parents' vacation would offer a slight reprieve from daily check-ins, but apparently, she couldn't avoid ongoing, close contact.

"I hear you're dating Dr. Evan Scott. What a nice surprise! I should leave town more often." Mom giggled.

"We're *not* dating." Trust Louanne. She had looped in Mom from two provinces away. "We had lunch together. That's all."

"You should think about going out with him, dear. From what I remember, he's a very smart and lively person. Louanne says he matured into quite a handsome man. Of course, we well know brains and personality count as much as looks."

"Mom, let's not talk about Evan. Did you visit Stanley Park and Granville Island?"

"Yes, they were both lovely."

Mom didn't elaborate on the sights around Vancouver. Her voice drifted like a cloud. Jayne braced herself for her next, unhelpful comment.

"Did you think about Aunt Patsy's generous offer?"

"No." Jayne swung upright, marched to the kitchen, and yanked open the fridge. She refused to give this topic her undivided attention. Using her free hand, she rummaged in the vegetable drawer, grabbed salad ingredients, and tossed them onto the counter. "Anything else, Mom?"

"Think about your teeth, dear. How's Cara? Of course, she's in good hands."

"I haven't seen her since Monday, but I'm sure she's fine." Regret pinched Jayne's heart like always when anyone mentioned Cara. Jayne twisted the kitchen faucet to fill a glass of water, positioned the glass a little off-center, and blasted herself in the face. Too agitated to laugh, she mopped her cheeks and the lenses of her glasses with a hand towel.

"Okay, Jaynie." Mom sighed and paused. "I'll let you go. Dad and I will wait for you to pick us up at the airport on Sunday. Only a few more days until I see you. Oh, and say hi to Evan for me." In the middle of a giggle, she clicked off the phone.

Jayne tossed her phone onto the kitchen counter. She selected a knife, chopped vegetables, and hit the cutting board with satisfying *thunks*. Tension released, she sighed. Her mother would never change.

After dinner, she stared at herself in the bathroom mirror. With her toothbrush poised, she opened her mouth, stretched her lips wide, and examined her teeth. When feeling positive, she viewed her angled teeth like happy partygoers—relaxed and carefree. Honestly, they made her appearance unique but not homely. Mom, on the other hand, saw only an eyesore and an embarrassment worse than a weedy lawn. Were her teeth really that bad?

After university, when that dog food sales rep—she refused to repeat his name—flirted with her at the pet store she managed, he caught her in a vulnerable place. A male admirer had sent plain Jayne Jones reeling off balance. At the time, she almost believed her recent change of spelling—adding a *Y* to spice up Jane—had worked, just like the *E* in *Anne of Green Gables*. How naïve she had been! Drawn into his liberal lifestyle, she had convinced herself she didn't need a commitment. Casual was okay.

When she learned she was pregnant, she nearly died of dismay. Admitting her life-changing mistake to her parents had twisted her emotions into knots of shame and flooded boxes of tissue. In no position to raise a child on her own, with encouragement from Mom and Dad, she chose the next best option. Now, joy and sorrow chased each other in her heart. Cara lit her world, but…if only the situation were different.

After years of reflection, she understood her low self-esteem started the whole sorry situation. She examined her face in the mirror. Her hair hung straight and glossy. Her hazel eyes, framed by classic glasses, shaded with warmth. The shape of her face and nose didn't display any obvious flaws.

She paced to the living room and peered out the window. In the dusky light, she spotted a V formation of Canada geese flying south, and she detected their faint honks drifting by. The predictability of nature and the seasons always comforted her with their familiar rhythms.

Should she accept or reject Aunt Patsy's offer? Growing up, she never lacked for the basics from her stay-at-home mom and plumber dad. But they didn't have money for extras like orthodontics. After university, student loans stretched her budget. These days, she focused on more important things than the state of her teeth.

Cara, Mallory, and Brad...the dogs at the shelter...the youth she mentored...they all consumed her time, energy, and heart. But now Evan had crept into her world. He derailed her routine, and she couldn't stop thinking about his shattered glasses, picnic lunch, and appealing grin. Mind whirling, she needed something familiar and calming to clear her head. Of course, she craved time with Cara. Before she changed her mind, she spun and raced to grab her phone.

"Hi, Jayne." Mallory picked up the call on the first ring.

"Can I come and read Cara a bedtime story?" Jayne held her breath.

"Of course. Bring Sally, too."

Mallory's voice held a smile. "See you soon." Jayne threw on a jacket, hooked Sally's leash, and dashed out the door. Life in Prairieville was supposed to be nice and simple. Now that she was reacquainted with Evan, why did she feel everything was so complicated?

****

On Friday evening, Evan, accompanied by Dudley, met a bunch of teens on the cracked sidewalk in front of the rec center. Tonight's program focused on community service.

"Hey, guys." Evan reined in Dudley. He figured most kids liked dogs, but he didn't want to scare anyone with an overeager, clumsy canine greeting.

A girl with long, brown hair knelt and threw her arms around the retriever.

He rewarded her with a fat, wet lick.

"Ooh, you act just like Sally." She tipped her head out of range.

Dudley flopped to the pavement and rolled onto his back.

The girl rubbed his furry stomach. Straightening, she glanced at Evan. "Jayne broke your glasses."

"Yep." Suddenly self-conscious, Evan hung back and waved the group inside. He followed the teens into a lobby decorated in fall colors.

"Are you a new youth leader?" A gangly boy with curly, red hair stopped and stared.

In a town where everybody knew almost everyone else, he stuck out as a newcomer. "I'm not sure. Brad asked me to help out tonight. My name's Evan."

"Cool. I'm Will." The boy tromped down the stairs. "Did you just move here?"

"Yeah, but I grew up in Prairieville."

"Cool. See ya later." He bolted ahead to catch up with his friends.

Evan bent and unhooked Dudley's leash.

Now free, the dog veered at an angle to reunite

with Sally. He wagged and frolicked in a circle.

Some of the nearby kids laughed and pointed.

Evan paused for an instant and inhaled the stuffy basement air mixed with the cool, fresh blast that followed him inside. The smell of worn runners, furry dogs, and hair gel wafted into a thick, murky scent. Nobody seemed to mind the rambunctious pair of retrievers, so he left them to play. He scanned the room. How would Jayne react when she spotted him? He'd watch for any hint of a smile.

"Glad you came." Brad breezed by. "I'll organize the kids in a minute and break them into work teams.

Would Jayne give him an equally warm greeting?

"I'm Tasha." A woman wearing a wide, red headband over her frizzy, black hair swept her gaze over Evan, blinked, and grinned. "I work at Adopt-a-Dog with Jayne. Some of the kids will volunteer there tonight."

"Pleased to meet you." He recognized Tasha as the woman with Jayne at the town council meeting. Her eyes shone dark and kind.

"They'll pet and play with the dogs for about an hour and then come back here for hot chocolate and cookies. Anyway, welcome to the team."

"You bet." He shook her hand and glanced over at Jayne. Had he already committed to the role? "Most of my contact with kids has been checkups and fevers, but I'm always up for a challenge."

"You chose the right place." She laughed and hustled over to join a group of giggling girls.

For the second time this week, the warm atmosphere welcomed him. He relaxed his shoulders and slid his hands into his jeans pockets. Spotting Jayne across the room, he edged in her general direction to say hello. Maybe she'd be glad to see him.

Jayne glanced over, squatted, and continued her conversation with Cara.

Even from a distance, he sensed a special, close connection.

Jayne set a gentle hand on the girl's cheek and drew her into a hug.

Then Cara wriggled free, skipped off, and threw her arms around Sally's neck.

Jayne popped up and scanned the room. She raised a hand in a small wave but didn't approach. Instead, she bustled toward Tasha, tapped her shoulder, and launched into an animated exchange.

Mallory soon joined the pair.

Maybe Jayne didn't mean to avoid him. She shared close ties with the people here. Still, heat prickled under his collar, and he scanned the room for someone available to chat. He didn't need to take offense or assume she wanted to avoid him. Maybe he shouldn't even pursue her. If he didn't get too close, he wouldn't be crushed if she pushed him away.

In the center of the room, Brad raised a hand.

One by one, the kids followed suit.

Smart approach. Raising a voice didn't work as well as a quiet signal.

Soon, the group trailed their voices to a murmur, then silence fell.

Cara was the only little girl present. She was likely here because her mom was a leader. The rest were an assortment of fidgety teens

Dudley sniffed, jostled, and gathered generous pats and hugs.

A wash of memories trickled back, and he smothered a smile. The kid wearing thick glasses and elbowing another guy reminded him of himself at that age—a bit geeky but not afraid to socialize. Most of the group wore blue jeans and hooded sweatshirts, and some of the girls overdid their eye makeup. He didn't notice a single tattoo.

"I'll divide you into two teams." Brad numbered off the kids. "Team one will come with Mallory and me to the care home. We'll play shuffleboard and card games with the residents."

Evan removed his hands from his pockets and tapped his palms on the outside of his thighs. If he wasn't assigned to the care home, he'd join Jayne and Tasha at the dog shelter. He worked with plenty of seniors and would be fine with either environment, but time with the dogs would be a lot more fun.

The kids exchanged glances and nodded. A couple of the guys shifted and frowned. The assignment probably wasn't their first choice.

"Team two will help Jayne, Tasha, and Evan at Adopt-a-Dog." Brad rotated to face the kids. "You'll give out treats and play with the dogs."

"Yay."

"Cool."

The kids on team two cheered and high-fived.

Evan joined the action. Raising a hand in a few high-fives, he felt more like part of the group than a stranger. He slid his gaze sideways and caught Jayne's glance.

She flushed and turned away.

Was she pleased or dismayed to spend more time in his charming company? He'd soon find out. "Come,

Dudley." He hooked the dog's leash.

Outside in the brisk breeze, Tasha led the way for team two.

Her manner was as efficient as a teacher on a school field trip.

The group straggled behind, laughing, jostling, and waving their arms.

Hunching his shoulders against the chill, Evan hung back and, next to Jayne and the dogs, brought up the rear.

"I don't want to lose anybody." Jayne raised a finger and counted.

"They keep you busy." He thrust an arm forward and pointed at the group of seven.

"Definitely." She stared ahead.

She didn't elaborate or lead the conversation to another topic. Normally, he would jump in to fill the silence. So many questions bubbled to the surface he had to clamp his lips to contain them. He glanced at her profile and felt a jump in his pulse. Her stiff posture and smooth expression shielded her feelings like a door. He needed to knock before entering.

"Come in." At Adopt-a-Dog, Jayne waved the team into the crowded office area.

The earthy smell of fur and kibble circulated around the space. Yellow walls brightened the atmosphere around a pair of tidy desks.

"Listen to the ground rules." She raised her voice over the sound of barking and whining. She made eye contact with every youth and brushed by Evan.

Beside her, Tasha planted hands on hips and blocked the entrance to the kennel area.

"Sanitize your hands on the way inside." Jayne

pointed toward a large bottle on the corner of a desk. "Do not tease the dogs. Move slowly. Offer a hand to sniff before you touch them. I'll open the play area, and you can toss balls or sit on the floor and give pats. Got it?"

The kids nodded and lowered their voices.

"Sally and Dudley, stay here. We don't need more confusion back there."

"Good dogs." Evan stroked both retrievers. "Don't take it personally you're not welcome."

Jayne flickered up the corners of her mouth, then flitted her gaze right by.

In the shelter, near the dogs, she relaxed her stiff posture and smiled more often. She exuded an air of confidence and pride in her work. Admiration travelled up his spine. He liked what he observed.

"Evan."

She delivered his name in a tone as sharp as a pointy stick.

"Are you ready?"

Abruptly, he realized he'd been lost in reverie and left behind by the group like the slightly forlorn Sally and Dudley. "Sorry, ma'am." He hustled to join the rest. "You caught me daydreaming." She probably had no idea—and didn't need to know—she was the subject. Scanning the rows of pens, he breathed the musky air, and a faint odor of antiseptic drifted by. Concern grabbed his stomach like a dog chomped a bone. He couldn't stand the idea of Dudley ever living in such a sad place.

Sharp yips, deep woofs, and kids' voices filled the space. The next hour promised fun, even if a little heartbreaking. He ushered dogs into the open play area and stooped to pet a wriggly spaniel. Laughing, he wiped a big, wet lick off his cheek. A dog could erase just about any worry.

"I'd like to adopt him." Laughing, one of the teens, Gavin, leaned and offered pats. "But my grandma's allergic."

"Bummer." Evan flopped onto the floor. He glanced at the boy, reminiscent of his teenage self with light hair and thick glasses.

Immediately, a black lab accosted him.

"Take it easy, buddy." He tipped back his head and laughed. He glanced at Gavin. "My dog, Dudley, is one of my best friends."

Jayne circulated, supervised the group, and coached Natalie.

The girl backed into a corner and clasped her hands to her chest, but, with Jayne's guidance, relaxed her arms and petted a poodle.

Evan studied Jayne's movements. In this familiar and well-loved place, she forgot she had an audience. Uninhibited, she bent, scooped up pups, doled treats, and filled water buckets. She lavished the dogs with hugs and kisses and even let her teeth peek out behind her smiles.

He tossed balls, but he bounced his gaze her way as fast as Dudley grabbed rawhide. Why wasn't she married? Not many people her age remained single. She must like kids. He filed his questions for another time.

"Hey, if you ever need someone to take Dudley for a walk—like if you go away or something—maybe I could do it?" Gavin sniffed, adjusted his glasses, and threw a rope toy.

"Good idea." Nodding, Evan petted a timid pup.

"Thanks. I'll keep your offer in mind." He took a full breath but needed fresh air. He didn't mind the doggy odor, but the images of an abandoned mutt and a kid who longed for a pet sucked the air right out of him.

Squelching his urge to escape outside, for the rest of the hour, he traced Jayne's path and interactions with the dogs and kids. "Glad I came." He stretched, brushed a glob of retriever slobber off his sleeve, and grinned at Jayne. "I feel safer here than playing dodgeball." Amusement fluttered across her face, and her reaction sent a warm burst into his chest.

"Time to walk back to the rec center." Tasha gave a couple of sharp claps to grab attention.

After Jayne ensured the group returned all the dogs to their stalls, washed hands, and gathered at the door, she led the way outside.

Evan inhaled deep breaths of the fresh air he craved, gave Dudley an extra pat, and left a piece of his heart inside the shelter. If the council spent an hour with the dogs, they might take a second glance at Jayne's proposal. A weight descended on his shoulders. He shouldn't cheer for the competition, but he cared for the cause—and its leader.

He quickened his steps, then slowed. If he bolted ahead to walk next to Jayne, he might scare her with his obvious interest. He settled for the appealing view of her trim figure hustling along. Her hair swung with every stride, and strands lifted and danced in the crisp, evening breeze.

"What grade are you in?" He meandered next to Gavin.

"Tenth." Gavin tilted sideways and ran a hand along Dudley's furry back. "I plan to be a doctor."

Straightening, he yanked up his baggy jeans.

High school felt forever away. Twelfth grade was the year he and Jayne shared an English class. An uneasy memory jumped to his mind and then dropped an icy chunk of guilt into the pit of his stomach. She had bailed him out of a tough essay assignment and cemented his spot as the top student. How could he have been so selfish? Jayne, too, had harbored big dreams. If she had earned the scholarship, she might be a veterinarian today. He had taken advantage of Jayne for his own gain, and he couldn't change the past. Chilled at the realization, he increased his pace, pounding his runners on the pavement.

Hurrying to match Evan's stride, Gavin tripped and stumbled but caught himself before he fell.

"Excellent." Evan glanced over. Did he deserve to be a role model? "Work hard, and you'll achieve your goal." Back at the rec center, he savored the cozy atmosphere. He settled at a round table with kids, swallowed hot chocolate, and devoured a handful of cookies. The warm drink dissolved a little of the cold truth he carried.

Tasha dashed over and rested a hand on his shoulder. "We really need another male chaperone for the youth retreat next weekend. Can we count you in?" She grabbed the handles of several empty mugs and lifted them onto a tray.

"Uh…" Evan glanced up. The right answer caught in his throat. Should he jump in and see what happened?

"You'll have loads of fun. I promise." Grinning, Tasha balanced the tray on one hand and added another empty mug.

"I'll check my schedule." His calendar was clear, but he'd consult Brad before he made a commitment. He didn't mind the idea, as long as Brad agreed he could be a good enough influence on the kids. Also, how would Jayne feel?

"Don't wait too long, brother." Tasha picked up the tray. "Time's ticking."

"I'll let you know." He shoved back his chair. Already, some of the kids had left. "Goodnight, everyone." He raised an arm in a general wave but paused on Jayne.

She sat between Natalie and Mallory with Cara on her knee. Smiling at the little girl, Jayne bumped her knees up and down in a pony ride.

Cara wiggled and giggled.

He crossed to the table in three long strides. "Goodnight, ladies."

"Thanks for helping tonight." Mallory flashed a thumbs-up.

"Now do you see why the dogs need more space?" Jayne glared over the top of Cara's head.

"I understand." Swallowing, he shifted under her intense gaze. The medical clinic proposal benefitted the whole town. But he agreed Jayne and the dogs displayed a burning need. "The council will carefully consider all options."

"See you Monday?" Mallory raised her eyebrows.

"Maybe." Evan raised a hand. He needed to talk more with Jayne. She still viewed him as a tough adversary. "See you later."

"Bye." Jayne lowered her gaze to the back of Cara's hair.

She said *goodbye*—not *see you later*. He received

no encouragement from her flat tone or furrowed brow. But he didn't survive medical school, his birth mother's rejection, and a broken marriage without a bucket of determination. Despite her standoffishness, did Jayne recognize any of his good qualities? How could he convince her to give him a chance?

Chapter 8

Sunday afternoon, soaking up the thin, autumn sunshine, Jayne raked the straggler leaves in the front yard of her tidy bungalow. Swishing and crackling sounds and a growing pile signalled progress. She'd hurry and finish the chore before she walked to the rec center for the retreat planning session. Later this afternoon, she would meet her parents at the Regina Airport and return home in time for dinner.

If she encountered Evan at the meeting, she'd welcome him in a friendly way, like he was any newcomer to the team, but she wouldn't extend any special treatment. He—and likely others—would only jump to conclusions. She hated to become the topic of town gossip. She squeezed the rake with full force. Why did he invade her thoughts so often?

Half an hour later, Cara ran to greet Jayne in the main hallway of the rec center.

Following the same theme as the autumn decorations in the entranceway, touches of artificial, fall foliage brightened doorframes on either side.

"Hi, Auntie Jayne." Cara grabbed her around the hips. "Mommy says you and Grandma Iris and Grandpa Greg can come to our house for dinner."

"Did she really?" Jayne admired her rosy cheeks and squatted for a full hug. She drank in the scent of fresh air radiating from her swishing ponytail and pink jacket, then stretched tall.

Kind and generous Mallory frequently extended invitations to their home. Jayne couldn't have chosen better parents for her daughter. They even fully embraced the name Jayne had chosen. Cara meant loved one, and Jayne couldn't love her darling daughter more.

Smiling, Mallory caught up. "Yes, really."

Cara clasped Jayne's hands and twisted into a jive move.

"Iris and Greg haven't seen Cara for two weeks," said Mallory. "I imagine they can't wait. I'm sure they missed you, too, Jayne."

"But not as much as this little sweetie." Jayne released a hand and spun her. "Mom called almost every day for updates. Thank you for being so considerate." Still holding onto Cara, she leaned forward and hugged Mallory with one arm. A rush of affection chased by envy dashed through her chest. "I'll bring dessert."

"Perfect." Mallory glanced down. "Come, Cara. Now that we dropped off Daddy at his meeting, we'll walk home." She tapped Jayne's forearm. "See you later."

"Jaynie." Louanne swished in the door and sidled close. "I'm glad to see you."

What brought *her* here? Jayne stiffened. The way Louanne lowered her voice signalled a topic she probably didn't want to hear.

"I emailed your mom and told her we ran into each other last week." Louanne flashed a wide smile.

"Yeah, Mom mentioned she'd heard." Jayne glanced over her shoulder. Where was Tasha? Louanne had a good heart and was a loyal friend to her mom, but she should mind her own business. The time with Evan meant nothing, didn't it? She felt badly about his broken glasses. Sally liked Dudley. Brad invited him to volunteer with the youth. Only circumstances threw them together. But why did the memories linger? "I'd like to chat, but I better excuse myself and join the meeting." Hot and cold with confusion, she needed to escape.

With a cool hand, Louanne squeezed Jayne's arm. "Didn't Brad tell you? He recruited me as the camp cook and weekend nurse."

"Oh. How fun." Jayne contained an eye roll and attempted to inject enthusiasm into her tone.

"Go ahead, Jaynie. Right after I make a quick call, I'll join you." She rooted in her purse for her phone.

"Okay." Jayne hustled down the hallway, then filled a mug at the coffee station just outside the meeting room. Steadying her mug, she entered and braked.

On the far side of the table, opposite Tasha and Brad, sat Evan.

"Hey." He raised a hand.

"Hi." Jayne plunked into the chair beside him. The force sloshed a small puddle of coffee onto the table. Rolling her lips inward, she grabbed a notepad and pen from her purse and mopped the mess with a tissue. She shouldn't be surprised to find Evan here, but why the commotion in her body?

"Long time no see." Evan chuckled.

Jayne choked out a sound that might have suggested amusement. This past week, she had spent time with him nearly every day—some of it tense and some of it okay. If she blocked several things from her mind, she might find him pleasant enough company. But he carried too many strikes against him for her taste.

High school was a long time ago, but nothing guaranteed she could trust him now. Maybe he had just practiced his best behavior all week. Of course, she also faced the rather large problem of his partnership in the clinic expansion plans. Besides those issues, she feared his reaction to learning she was Cara's birth mother. Many people judged someone with a less-than-perfect past, and a lot of guys wouldn't accept such a non-traditional arrangement with a child. What a confusing muddle! Clearly, avoiding him would be easier than risking her feelings. But why did her heart beat so erratically?

"What's for lunch?" Evan rubbed his stomach.

"I heard you arranged the food." Tasha laughed and shook her shoulders. She tightened her frizzy, black ponytail. "Bring it on."

"Sorry. I missed that detail." Evan shrugged and gulped a mouthful of coffee. "Which is unfortunate because I can't stand to miss a meal. Right, Jayne?" He laughed and pumped his elbow in the air like he might prod her for an answer.

"Uh, sure. Whatever you say, Evan." Jayne widened her eyes.

Tasha flickered a smile across the table.

Even though Tasha teased about Evan, she sympathized with Jayne's discomfort and understood the whole story of Cara. Darting her gaze to the doorway, Jayne bit her tongue. Louanne frequently arrived late. She glanced at her watch. She needed to hit the road to the airport by two p.m.

"Hi, guys and gals." Louanne breezed in, scanned the room, and dropped into a chair at the end of the table. "I hope I didn't make you wait too long."

"Let's get started." Brad tapped his pen and ran a hand over his bristly head. "We'll meet at the rec center at four on Friday. Twenty youth confirmed they'll participate."

"Ooh. A busy weekend." Louanne rested her forearms on the table.

"I rented two vans to transport everybody." Brad referred to a list. "I'll drive one. Who wants to drive the other?"

"Not me." Louanne sat back. "Thanks, but no thanks."

"Ride with me, Louanne." Brad made a note. "With all your lunch program experience, you know how to keep kids in line."

"Well, if you insist." Louanne leaned in and clasped her hands. "Kids, food, and bandages are my specialty. I only hope I don't have to administer any first aid."

"How about a volunteer for the other van?" Brad scanned the group.

Jayne paused. She'd really rather not take responsibility for driving ten boisterous teens on the highway to a camp about an hour away. Doodling on her notepad, she swallowed and shifted her gaze between Tasha and Evan. She couldn't appear timid or incapable, especially in front of him, so if needed, she would accept the challenge.

"I will." Tasha shot up a hand. "Let me behind the wheel, and watch out, kids." She laughed and steered an imaginary bus in daring curves. "But only if Jayne or Evan rides along. Somebody else can worry about the kids, and I'll keep these eyes on the road." Using two fingers, she pointed at both eyes, then flipped her hand toward an imaginary highway ahead.

"Why don't you both ride with Tasha?" Louanne winked. "Brad and I can handle the other van."

"You beat Jayne to the idea, Louanne." Evan snapped his fingers and swooped his hand. "I can tell by her smile she's pretty excited."

"Ha." Jayne flushed and rolled her eyes. "If you only knew…" Take that, Evan. He could interpret her remark as he wanted. "I'll ride with Tasha. You…" She shot Evan a sharp glance. "You take your pick."

She imagined the conversation between her mother and Louanne. They'd giggle like school girls about Louanne's attempted matchmaking and Jayne's discomfort. The pair yearned to see her settle down with an eligible bachelor like Evan. She leaned back, crossed an arm over her middle, balanced an elbow on the folded arm, and rested her fingertips on her mouth.

Across the table, Tasha widened her eyes and shrugged.

"I'll ride with you charming women." Grinning, Evan flicked his eyebrows. "To make your day."

"Wait a minute." Tasha glanced at Jayne. "More like the other way around, brother. We'll grace you with our company. Right, Jayne?"

"Right." Jayne grabbed her notepad and drew it to her chest like a shield. Should she join in the lighthearted joking? Evan's banter was harmless enough.

"You three sort out who gets the better deal." Brad

chuckled and checked his list of things to cover. "Now, food. Louanne graciously offered to prepare the menus and meals."

"True, but I told Brad I won't lug a bunch of groceries." She scanned their faces. "Whoever shops should zip into Prairie Market in Regina to get larger quantities than our local Felix Foods carries. Felix will understand."

Jayne agreed. She supported local businesses and, most of the time, shopped in Prairieville, but sometimes, she bought things in Regina.

"Who wants the job?" Brad used his pen as a pointer and circled the group.

"I'm busy with my kids' activities and homework, so I can't leave town to shop." Tasha shook her head. "Sorry, guys."

"You or me?" Evan cocked his head toward Jayne. "Or you *and* me. Could be fun."

"Good idea." Louanne nodded and slapped her hands together in a single smack.

"I volunteer." Jayne half raised a hand. Mentally, she reviewed her week's plans. Other than attending the youth group on Monday, she'd focus on rallying support for the Adopt-a-Dog expansion. She could spare a few hours to shop—on her own. She didn't need a guy's help, especially from Evan. In a vehicle together, she'd need to make conversation all the way to and from Regina. What if he broached topics she'd rather avoid?

"I'll help." Evan flexed his arms. "Don't refuse my muscle power."

"But…" A flush crawled from Jayne's neck to her cheeks, and she lowered her gaze to the table. How could she decline without seeming rude? The thirty-minute ride both ways would stretch forever. Could her heart handle the stress?

"Okay, that detail is settled. Thanks for volunteering, Jayne and Evan." Brad checked off another item. "You work out the logistics. Now, moving on to activities, I drafted most of the schedule."

"I'll help." Tasha grinned and poked a thumb into the center of her chest. "Fun is my middle name. Just tell me what you need. I grabbed a better job than you, girl." She glanced at Jayne.

Jayne shrugged and wrinkled her nose. "You don't hold the licence on fun." She might not rival Tasha's enthusiasm for everything, but she held her own with Cara and the teenage girls. She clamped her lips into a tight smile, and the heat in her cheeks intensified. Evan wanted to hang out with her. Why was he so interested? More puzzling, why did she even care?

****

Later that afternoon, Evan tapped on the red front door of Brad and Mallory's white, two-story home.

Cara swung it wide open. "Hi. You're Evan." She bounced and rustled her dress. "He's Dudley."

"Righto, missy." He grinned and nodded. She was a cute little thing with brown hair tied in thin pigtails and her wide eyes blinking behind pink glasses. Maybe one day, he'd parent a child of his own. If he ever became a father, he'd treasure the opportunity. He whooshed out a deep breath like a football hit him in the gut. He'd never abandon a child—unlike his birth mother. "May I come in?" Shifting, Evan waited for her answer.

Dudley didn't pause for an invitation, wriggled

ahead, and licked Cara's cheek.

"Okay." She giggled and hugged the dog around his neck.

In a moment, Mallory, wearing a flowing blouse and matching pants, swished up behind Cara. "I'm glad you could join us for dinner." She was as warm and welcoming as the casual, neutral surroundings.

Voices drifted from the living room to the entranceway, and the delicious aroma of garlic-seasoned roast beef encircled him. When Brad invited him for Sunday dinner, he didn't mention other guests, but Evan didn't mind. He needed to re-establish ties with the community and meet new people, too. He rounded the corner into the living room and stopped short.

Sitting cross-legged on the beige carpet, Jayne brushed a doll's hair. Glancing up, she widened her eyes.

Her fuzzy, light-brown sweater blended with the furnishings.

A middle-aged man and woman, who must be Jayne's parents, leaned forward on the couch. Her mom wore round glasses with gold frames, and her hair hung to chin length. The color was brown like her look-alike daughter's shade but streaked with gray. The couple must enjoy a closeness to Brad's family, too.

"Evan." The man leapt to his feet. "I'm Greg Jones, Jayne's dad. I remember you from high school. You grabbed all the major awards."

"Hello." Evan stuck out a hand. "Not all, but a few. Feels like a hundred years ago." Did Greg need to remind him? Evan already felt like a schmuck, and the guilt residing in his stomach throbbed. Maybe Jayne and not Evan had deserved the financial boost.

"I'm Iris." She blinked and held out her hand. "So nice to see you again. I heard you returned to Prairieville."

He better elaborate to satisfy her curiosity. Under her scrutiny, he felt like a specimen in a lab. "I like the concept of an expanded healthcare center. I also dislike big-city life. So Prairieville called." He didn't mention the deep hurt and bad memories he wanted to escape.

"We meet again." Jayne glanced at Evan, then offered the doll to Cara. "I like her pretty curls."

Brad bounded into the room. "Hey, Evan. I just carved the roast. I'll send Dudley to the backyard to play with Sally."

Evan scanned the spacious room for a spare chair and chose the cream-colored loveseat across from Jayne's parents.

Greg settled onto the sofa again.

"How's your mom?" Iris leaned forward.

Her question was innocent, but something in her tone reminded him of an investigative reporter. "Fine, thank you." Of course, Iris had known his mom during his childhood years before she relocated to Victoria. Probably, they had attended school meetings and drunk coffee together. Her interest in his mom was natural. But now, would she pry into his past?

"How's business?" Greg rubbed together his big, calloused hands. "Never a shortage of sick people." He chortled.

Evan remembered him as a friendly dad. He had coached kids' baseball, and once, he even checked Evan's parents' furnace at no charge. Over the years, his build had grown stockier, and his hair thinned and grayed. "So far, so good." Evan chuckled and slapped his palms on the arms of the chair. "Considering my partner shifts all the tough cases to me. Right, bud?" He timed his friendly jab to coincide with Brad's reappearance.

"Yeah, right." Brad laughed. "Why do you think I lured you here?"

"Maybe you should add a dentist to your clinic. Here's an interesting tidbit." Iris lowered her voice and glanced from Jayne to Evan. "Jaynie's aunt offered to pay the cost of orthodontics to get those pesky front teeth straightened. Isn't that news exciting?"

"Mom, stop." Gripping the doll brush, Jayne glared at her mother. "Please, don't share private information." She clamped her lips. "You don't have the right." Sudden silence draped the room. He wanted to scold indiscreet Iris and hug poor Jayne. Her face shaded pink, then white. She probably didn't appreciate the childish nickname, either. *His* mom wasn't perfect, but she would never embarrass him in public.

After a pause, Jayne resumed her game with Cara.

What could he say or do to make the situation less awkward?

Just then, from the backyard, loud woofs reverberated into the living room. Evan rocked out of the chair. "Excuse me for a minute. I hear Dudley barking. I better tell him to be quiet before the neighbors complain." Straightening, he smirked. "Oh, right. I *am* one of the neighbors."

Iris tilted off the sofa and patted Jayne's shoulder.

Jayne shrugged off the touch.

How could a mother with so little tact have produced such a restrained and sensitive daughter? He hurried to the back door to quiet Dudley. He'd spare Jayne the embarrassment of his witnessing any more of the scene.

"Come to the table, everyone." Mallory waved toward the dining area.

Fortunately, the call to dinner broke the tension, at least, temporarily. Evan followed the others into the dining room. The space flowed from the living room and held the same warm appeal. Placemats in autumn tones and a low bouquet of chrysanthemums decorated the table.

"Sit here by Grandma." Iris leaned and tapped the seat of the chair to her right.

Cara lowered her gaze and slid it to Mallory. "Can I sit by Auntie Jayne?"

"How about if you sit between Grandma Iris and Auntie Jayne?" Mallory helped Cara hop into her place.

Obviously, the group considered themselves family. Evan hung back until Brad assigned him the spot at the end of the table, next to Jayne. He'd keep his knees and feet directly in front of the chair so he didn't bump her, in case she thought he did it on purpose. Her stiff posture suggested for now, he better stick to a cordial but detached approach. His common sense agreed, but apparently, reason did not enter into his feelings for Jayne.

Mallory passed a platter of meat and bowls of vegetables, then tilted her head toward Cara. "If you want dessert, missy, you need to eat a little of everything."

Cara scrunched her nose and glanced at Jayne.

Jayne smiled with her lips barely parted and nodded.

Cara sighed and separated her different food items so nothing touched.

The interactions between the two stood out. Their bond shone as bright as a sunshiny day and warmed his insides like a bowl of chicken noodle soup.

Cara leaned so close she bumped Jayne's elbow.

Glancing down, Jayne gently straightened her and then concentrated on her plate.

Did she wish for a child of her own, too? With her close contact and loving approach with Cara, she would be a natural mom. In the midst of the caring circle, a sudden burst of loneliness punched his chest. Maybe someday, he would host Sunday dinners at his table, surrounded by a wife and children. With his mother so far away, no siblings, a runaway ex-wife, and a birth mother who forgot him for twenty-five years, he lacked special people in his life. Even with an irritating mother, Jayne was luckier than she might believe. Iris showed her love in an inappropriate way, but she cared. He exhaled a full breath, sawed the meat, and stabbed a large bite.

"Hey, give me the report on the council meeting." Greg swigged water and pointed his fork from Brad to Evan and then Jayne. "Bit of a showdown?"

"Uh, let's avoid that topic right now." Jayne set down her fork and raised her napkin to her lips.

Wow. What next? Both parents had floated hot topics, and no doubt, Jayne was not impressed.

"A while back, Jayne and I agreed to disagree on what to do with the vacant lot." Brad darted his gaze from her to Evan.

"I won't talk about differences of opinion now. She might throw peas at us." Evan held up a hand like a baseball mitt in front of his face.

Cara jerked up her head and giggled. "I'll help."

"Evan just meant to be funny." Grandma Iris tapped Cara's plate. "Eat up now, sweetie."

"You heard council deferred a decision." Jayne directed her gaze at Greg.

Her tone rang firm and final. Under the circumstances, everybody better tread carefully.

"Hey, Jaynie," said her dad, "No need to get your shirt in a knot." He widened his eyes, then winked at Brad.

Jayne clamped her lips and chewed. Narrowing her eyes, she concentrated on her plate.

"The mayor wanted to get home to cheer for the Prairie Winters on TV." Evan swished a piece of meat in gravy. He had expected a pleasant Sunday dinner and not one where tension simmered. Still, since Greg had been out of town and missed the meeting, he just showed a natural interest. He cared about the outcome for his daughter's passion. But the topic was definitely a sore point with Jayne.

"Yup, that's Tommy all right." Greg rested a forearm on the table. "You can give me the details later, Jayne."

She nodded and shifted her gaze from side to side.

Did Jayne wish for an escape route? "Fantastic meal. Toast to the hosts." Evan raised his water class. Glancing around the table, he caught Jayne's gaze and sensed she relaxed her stiff cheek muscles for an instant. Maybe she appreciated his attempt to divert the topic. If only he could tell her he was an ally and not a foe.

Later, for Jayne's sake, he'd talk to Brad about

options for the expansion plan. Right now, he'd float non-confrontational topics. He smiled and swivelled to clink glasses with Greg. The guy likely had no idea how intriguing Evan found his daughter. Just days away, the shopping trip for the youth retreat supplies could prove very interesting.

Chapter 9

A few days later, Evan watched out the front window of his place for Jayne's arrival. "I'll see you in a couple of hours, Dudley." Evan gave the dog a vigorous rub. She had refused his offer to drive to Regina for the food supplies and insisted on taking her vehicle. Either way, he'd occupy himself for an evening and, better yet, get to know her better. He'd readily agreed Jayne could pick him up at six o'clock.

With no sign of her vehicle out front, he hustled to the bathroom mirror, ran his hands over his hair, straightened his glasses, and flashed a practice grin. Most times, his jovial manner was genuine, but an undercurrent of uncertainty circled him like a wasp. Jayne sent cool vibes, so would she reject him like his ex-wife? Nobody could sooth the worst hurt of all. His birth mother didn't even want to meet him until way too late. His adoptive mom—his true mom—had always lavished him with love and attention, but she couldn't change the circumstances of his birth.

Back at the front window, he rotated and scanned the living area. Not that he'd invite somebody to view his rented home anytime soon, but he surveyed the place through outsider's eyes. The owner had renovated and removed a wall to create an open plan, combined the former kitchen and living room, and added an island to update the cooking and seating areas. Beige tile backed the sink, and open counter space stretched long enough for a couple of work stations. Even a legitimate cook would be impressed. He didn't quite qualify for that category. The scent of his quick dinner of grilled cheese sandwiches lingered.

Caramel-colored walls united the whole area, and his furniture matched. A dark-brown, leather couch and loveseat framed a beige-and-brown area rug. A few unpacked boxes waited stacked in a corner. The whole effect was casual and comfortable.

A light honk out front grabbed his attention, and he rubbed Dudley one last time. "Be good. I'll see you later."

Dudley groaned, flopped to the floor, and rested his chin on a front paw.

The dog had greeted patients at work all day, so he could nap for a few hours. Dashing to the car, Evan zipped his jacket. Still pleasant for mid-October, the air hinted of an evening chill closing in. Fortunately, the forecast looked okay for this coming weekend and should allow outdoor activities and evening bonfires at camp.

"Good evening, Miss Jones." He yanked open the car door and hopped into the passenger seat. "I appreciate your chauffeur services this fine evening." The spotless, black interior of her sport utility vehicle smelled of polish.

"Hello, Dr. Scott." She waited for him to buckle his seatbelt. "Where to this evening? I should warn you I charge premium rates after six p.m."

She actually played along with his joking, formal tone and squished her cheeks upward into some semblance of a close-mouthed smile. "I hope I can afford the return trip." He laughed and glanced over to gauge her reaction. "You better not leave me stuck in Regina."

"Hmmm. Don't tempt me." She pulled away from the curb and steered toward the highway.

He chuckled and focused ahead. This evening might offer as much fun as he hoped. When he had volunteered to help shop, he couldn't miss her grimace, like she suffered a sudden headache. But now, she relaxed a little and, apparently, had resigned herself to spending a couple of hours together.

Gravel tapped against the car along the narrow feeder road.

"Feels okay back in Prairieville." He scanned out the windshield. Most of the grain harvest was complete, but bales dotted the fields on either side. Like most small towns in Saskatchewan, Prairieville depended on crops to support its economy. When farmers did well, their efforts helped everyone thrive. Of course, medical services were always much needed and available at no cost through Canada's universal Medicare, so they never dipped in demand.

"Would you have returned without the health clinic expansion plans?" Jayne kept her gaze fixed on the road ahead. She lowered the volume of the folk music strumming in the background.

Her voice switched from verging on warm to chilled with ice chips. She didn't hide the fact she resented the competitive bid. If the medical center proposal won, it would impact her mission to create a better facility for the dogs. She had reason for concern. Evan and Brad formed a formidable team with a clear, achievable vision. Residents deserved and valued first-class health-care services.

But Jayne presented plenty of justification for her plan, too. The animal lovers in town supported an expanded shelter to keep dogs safe, warm, and well fed. Healthier people or happier dogs? The town council would decide. The choice wouldn't be easy, and Jayne would chase her dream like Dudley chased a squirrel.

Both proposals held merit. Animals deserved a fair chance in life, too. He stared out the window like the answer would appear in the sunset. Still, in simple terms, Jayne's proposal was chicken broth compared to his and Brad's meaty stew. Both met a need, but health care likely filled a deeper hunger in the people of Prairieville. If the council viewed things his way, he would alienate Jayne—maybe forever.

The tires hummed along the highway, and a bump in the pavement jolted him out of his reverie. Back to Jayne's question, would he have returned to Prairieville without the proposed medical center dangling as a carrot? "Not likely." He had yearned for a fresh start but could have found it in many places across the country. The opportunity to form part of a comprehensive medical team appealed, along with the chance to invest in a community and make it stronger. He also felt an inexplicable pull to return to his roots.

"If you don't receive approval, will you leave?" She clenched the wheel.

"Never." His definitive answer surprised him as much as Jayne.

Staring ahead, she shifted and widened her eyes.

She hadn't expected his ongoing commitment to Prairieville. Maybe she believed he left once, so he'd do it again. Possibly, she even hoped he'd depart.

"Prairieville needs more people who are willing to step up and make a difference. So many of us moved away after graduation, we left a gap." Evan studied her gentle profile with its small nose, thin cheeks, and smooth skin. Within days, he had realized he belonged here, where people noticed and needed him.

"I agree." Jayne focused her gaze ahead.

"The youth group is desperate for volunteers." Chuckling, he studied her profile. "If they'll take me, they'll take anybody."

"You're right." A light chortle escaped her lips, but just as quickly, she resumed her flat expression.

He blinked and swallowed. Joking or not, her response hurt. Shades of things to come?

****

"Do you think you'll stay in Prairieville?" Evan glanced over.

"Yes." She'd never leave Cara. Should she explain? Would he judge or understand? She opened her mouth and closed it. Uncertainty blocked her words like a fence. All things considered, she belonged in her hometown. She was lucky Louanne hadn't blurted the whole, sad story on the corner in front of the café or at the youth group meeting.

Jayne rolled her lips inward, sealing an envelope of secrets. Why couldn't she totally forgive herself? Whenever she explained the situation and her closeness with Mallory, Brad, and Cara, she waited for a shadow to darken the conversation. She knew what people thought. How could she give up her beautiful child to someone else's care, and how did she manage the unorthodox arrangement? Sometimes, she wondered the same things, too. "I…uh…" Should she elaborate?

Nothing surprised a doctor, did it? Her personal life was really none of his business, and she didn't need to feel ashamed. But still…

Suddenly, the car thunked and swerved.

Groaning, she jostled in her seat and tightened her hands around the wheel.

"What the heck?" Evan grabbed the armrest.

She huffed, hit the brakes, and skidded to a stop on the shoulder. "Probably a flat tire. Just what I need." The prairie stretched wide around them in a shrinking spotlight.

"I've changed a few tires. You got a jack and a spare?" Evan grabbed the handle and threw open the door.

"In the back. I've changed more than one tire, too, so I don't need you to rescue me. But thanks, anyway." At age sixteen, after she passed her driver's licence test, she learned the basics of car maintenance and troubleshooting. Thanks to her dad's coaching, she knew how to check the oil, boost a dead battery, and change a tire.

"You just wanted to spend extra time with me, right?" Evan smothered a smile.

She couldn't help giggling. With his large, hopeful eyes and quick, wide grin, he reminded her of a little boy asking permission to stay up past his bedtime. He had matured from the self-centered, high school student who insulted her teeth, stole her chance at a scholarship, and crushed her heart.

Even so, she wasn't ready to expose her secrets or her questionable history. Guys didn't necessarily want a child. For sure, they didn't want a woman with baggage so heavy it was hard to lift. Guys didn't want a woman like her. Huffing, she blinked away the unsettling thoughts, opened the door, and hopped out of the car. "Here I go."

"Here *we* go." He leapt out and met her at the hatch. "We'll throw on the spare tire and continue on our way."

"Good thing the trouble happened before total darkness." She scanned the sky and absorbed the sunset. It glowed the color of fire with a bucket of royal-blue water ready to douse the flames.

He assembled the jack. "I'll pump, and you sing."

"Sing?" She nearly choked at his offbeat sense of humor. The image of belting out a tune on the side of the road struck her as funnier than anything she'd heard since…well, in a very long time.

"Yeah. While I handle the grunt work, I expect you to keep me amused."

"I can change my own tire." She placed a hand on a hip. "Besides, I can't sing a note. You might run away and force me to shop alone." She better rein in her amusement, or she might suggest she really liked him.

"If you owe me, you'll need to return the favor by joining me for dinner." Evan puffed his breath into the evening air.

She hoisted the spare out of the back and grabbed the tire iron. "Who said anything about dinner?" She couldn't possibly agree to a real date—not when she viewed him as stiff competition and not when she wasn't at ease with the past. She'd keep their contact cordial—two volunteers doing the right thing for the youth group.

Gritting her teeth, she loosened the bolts. She had hoped to complete the errand within two hours, drop off

Evan, and continue rallying support for her proposal. This delay would add another thirty minutes to the trip and cut into her valuable free time.

Slipping in so close he nearly bumped her elbow, he slid the jack into place and pumped. "I'll cook seafood linguine at my place. You can even bring Sally. Dudley will welcome the female company."

Jayne drew in a sharp breath of his cool, clean scent, and it sent a tug of attraction into her middle. Why did she react like she wanted more? "Thanks for the offer, but I don't like seafood." She furrowed her brow. Actually, she didn't mind the flavor.

"I'll substitute chicken." He grunted, straightened, and stretched. "Or lasagna."

"You don't give up, do you?" She parted her lips into a smile, then jammed them together.

"Who's more stubborn? You or me?" He removed the flat tire.

She rolled the spare into place. "I'm not stubborn." She stared at the rubber treads to avoid landing her gaze on his fitted jeans. Despite joking about his less-than-perfect physique, he deserved a second look.

He snorted. "No, of course not."

"I'm determined." He didn't have the right to label her anything. She didn't run an efficient dog shelter without an abundance of tenacity. Without brave perseverance, after her unplanned pregnancy, she wouldn't have rebuilt a life. Determination would help her succeed in her expansion proposal. But she'd need an extra measure of grit to lock the door on Evan.

"Stubborn." Grinning, he backed away.

"I'm not..." Why argue? She wouldn't give him the satisfaction of getting riled over his assessment. She would rise above the hot button and brush off his comments.

"Pass the wrench." He cranked on the bolts.

She hoisted the damaged tire into the trunk, wiped her hands on her jeans, and waited for him to lower the car into place. If he insisted on pitching in, he could save her some of the work. "Thanks for your help." She plopped back into the driver's seat, slammed the door, and glanced over.

"No problem." He grinned and buckled his seatbelt. "You can thank me over dinner."

She sighed and straightened her expression. Why give him hope, which would only encourage him to try harder? He might as well learn now not to waste his time. But why did his presence make her pulse jump? She rode in silence for a few kilometers, except for the drumming of his fingers on the armrest, and she mentally reviewed the shopping list she had compiled.

"Should we divide and conquer?" Evan paused the tapping and glanced over.

Did he read her mind? "Good idea." If she assigned him half the list, she'd save time. Apart, she could spend a few peaceful minutes regrouping without his banter.

"As long as I'm allowed to buy plenty of hotdogs and marshmallows, I'm good." He patted his stomach. "Deer." He jerked up a hand to point.

"I see." She eased off the gas pedal and gripped the wheel. She had already spotted the animal along the side of road, and she positioned her foot ready to brake. Dusk in the country was a prime time for wildlife, and she never fully relaxed at the wheel.

"Just wanted to make sure. Deer dart fast."

"Yeah. They sure do." Extra vigilance helped. Accidents happened so quickly, and she frequently spotted dead wildlife on the highway. She shuddered and turned up the music to discourage more conversation. Focused on the road, she listened to folksy vocals mixed with the hum of tires. Fifteen minutes later, she steered into the parking lot of the grocery store at North City Mall. Outside, chilly wind whipped her hair across her cheeks and rustled Evan's jacket.

"Give me half the list, and I'll race you." Hustling toward the store door, Evan rubbed his hands together.

"Race me?" Did he find fun in everything?

"Yup. You'll be surprised how fast I can knock off a grocery list." Evan stuck out his hand.

"If you're sure." She tore the list in two and, inside the store, squinted under the bright lights. A blast of warm air tamed the outside chill. The sweet scent of sugar cookies tempted, but she couldn't spare time for a treat.

"On your mark, get set, go." Clanging a cart, he bolted toward the snack aisle.

She paused, then grabbed a cart and sped in the opposite direction. No way would she concede a win. She dodged other shoppers and sniffed the scents of strawberries, oranges, and tomatoes in the produce section.

"I'm ahead." Zipping by her on the canned goods aisle, he pointed at the pile in his cart.

She couldn't help but giggle. The sooner she completed the shop, the better. So *what* if he believed he won? Breathing quicker, she increased her speed, narrowly missing an elderly woman who plastered herself against a shelf. Up and down several aisles, she didn't catch sight of him, and she nearly completed her list. Rounding the end of a cereal display at a blind corner, she rammed her cart directly into his in a head-on collision. The *crash* reverberated down the aisle, and she cringed.

Several shoppers paused and stared.

"Ouch," he shouted and grinned. "You don't need to get ugly about your impending loss. I hope you didn't break any eggs."

"Sorry about the accident." She wheeled past him for the home stretch. Scanning the cookie aisle, she spied graham crackers on the bottom shelf and dove to snatch six boxes. Without a pause, she zoomed to the checkouts.

Grinning in lane two, he unloaded his cart like an efficient robot.

Quickly, gauging the options, she avoided the self-checkout and chose the cashier with the shortest line. Waiting for the man ahead to pay, she stacked items on the conveyor belt.

A few tills over, Evan bobbed his head forward and back, emptying his cart.

She could catch up. Of course, she could beat him. "I'm a bit rushed." She plopped four bags of marshmallows next to ten loaves of bread.

"Okay." The cashier, a young woman with tattooed arms, yawned and swiped a bag of apples.

Jayne gripped the cart handle. This race was silly. She shouldn't care if Evan finished first. But something about his lopsided grin and twinkly eyes made her want to beat him. She shot the cart forward and grouped similar items to speed the process.

The cashier nodded but kept a steady pace. When she lifted the ground beef, she left a streak of pink fluid on the countertop and paused to wipe the mess.

Tapping a toe, Jayne glanced over her shoulder and spotted Evan. He hadn't left the checkout. She still had a chance. Several agonizing minutes later, she paid and charged toward the door.

Munching on a chocolate bar, Evan leaned on his cart. "Finally."

"How did you beat me?" He acted like he'd waited forever. She huffed but laughed inside. With puffed chest under a navy-blue sweater and jean jacket, he resembled a kid who just scored a winning goal. Although irritating, he deserved credit for shopping in record time. Alone, at normal speed, she would have taken more than twice as long.

"Pure skill." He crinkled the candy wrapper and tossed it into the cart. "I'll explain my technique on the way home."

"You're lucky I won't make you walk." She steered outside at a brisk pace, slightly in the lead.

He burst ahead and passed her "Speed-walking race you to the car." He grinned over his shoulder. "You can't beat me."

The guy never quit. She wanted to resist, but why not play along, just this once? Still, all the way, a nagging question chased her through the parking lot and buzzed like a fly in her brain. Should she just relax and enjoy the fun? His zany humor and good-natured banter tempted her like candy. What if she couldn't resist? Her heartbeat skittered from the crazy race…and something else. Puffing, she touched the tailgate of the car just seconds behind him. "Okay, enough. I admit you won."

She swung up the hatch and loaded groceries.

"Yeah. With a little practice, you'll improve." Smirking, he heaved several bags into the trunk.

"Sure, Evan. Beginner's luck." She attempted a serious tone, but she heard amusement spill into her voice. Now, he'd know she enjoyed his company, which probably wasn't a good thing. Her reaction would only encourage him. He was nice enough and plenty attractive, but he still belonged at a distance, didn't he?

Her face burned, even though a crisp wind bit her ears. While she closed the tailgate, she bowed her head, then rounded the car to the driver's seat. If he noticed her pink cheeks, maybe he'd think they had colored in the cold air. He couldn't really be the cause, could he?

Now, she just had to survive the trip home. With any luck, she would steer clear of both unpredictable wildlife and probing conversation. For the next thirty minutes, could she make sure he didn't tread into territory she'd rather avoid?

Chapter 10

"Ready, girl?" Two days later, on Friday afternoon, Tasha locked the shelter door and jingled her ring of keys.

"All set." Jayne flipped up the collar on her camel-colored jacket against the autumn chill. Whenever she left total responsibility for the shelter to someone else, she always nursed a slight nervous twitch in her stomach. While she spent the weekend away with the youth, she'd rely on dedicated volunteers to care for the dogs. Today, the feeling intensified to a nagging squeeze. The teens didn't concern her, but one of the other volunteers most certainly did.

After shopping, the trip home with Evan had been pretty uneventful. Maybe prompted by the presence of a carful of groceries, Evan entertained her with stories of his last visit with his mother. She had cooked, baked, and stuffed him with so much good food he gained five pounds in a week.

"Happy to help, ma'am." After unloading the groceries at her place, Evan gave Sally a vigorous rub and backed outside. "Dudley will be jealous."

"Thanks again." She had shut the door and leaned against the inside until her sprinting heartbeats slowed and Sally coaxed her to play. Why did he cause this surprising effect?

"Jayne, did you hear what I said?"

She blinked and dragged her focus back to Tasha.

"I'll grab my kids and suitcase and meet you at the rec center in an hour." Tasha lifted an arm in a half wave and headed to the rental van parked in front of the shelter.

"See you soon." With Sally trotting by her side, Jayne hustled toward home. She'd drop off the dog at her parents' place and gather her things. She and Tasha had already loaded the food, packed in coolers, during their noon break.

Passing assorted shops and Sam's, she mentally reviewed the activities organized for the youth. Games like *Capture the Flag* and *Alligator Swamp* always promoted lots of action and laughter.

No doubt, Evan would jump right in like one of the kids. Why couldn't she force him from her mind? Even all day Thursday, she had wrestled her thoughts from him so she could concentrate on work. With great effort, she contacted individual donors and major sponsors for increased support, and she received a positive response from nearly everyone. If she convinced enough people to lobby the town council, she might succeed. By the end of the day, she had nursed a mild headache and not even Tasha's enthusiastic reassurance had made her feel any better. The decision could tip either way.

Now, while Jayne regrouped for the weekend ahead, she veered toward the open field at the edge of town to exercise Sally. No doubt, Brad and Evan rallied their supporters, too. She stiffened, and unkind thoughts crawled like ants throughout her brain. Just as quickly, she squashed her negativity. It only wasted valuable energy.

At the youth retreat, she'd need to lock away bitterness and focus only on the purpose of the weekend. As a role model for the teens, she couldn't strike out against the competition, even if she was tempted. She needed to work together with Brad and Evan and accept a resolution that would benefit the community. The idea was easier said than done. Whatever happened, she needed to maintain a strong relationship with the adoptive father of her daughter and—really?—tread softly on her growing bond with Evan.

"Come, Sally." Jayne slapped her palms on her thighs, braced herself for the clumsy bump against her leg, and continued her walk. The bright sunshine and crackle of leaves underfoot lightened her load and sparked a glimmer of anticipation for the youth event. Interacting with so many people throughout multiple activities, she likely wouldn't even find herself close to Evan. She could easily dodge him, choose a dinner seat at another table, and park between others at the campfire. Deep in thought, within minutes, she bounded up the steps of her parents' tidy, yellow bungalow.

Dad swung open the front door and petted the dog. "Hi, Jayne. Hey, Sal Gal."

The air inside wafted the delicious aroma of chocolate chip cookies. "Thank you for your help." She had no qualms about leaving her beloved retriever with her parents. They loved Sally almost as much as she did.

"Have fun, dear." From behind, Mom popped her head around Dad. "Enjoy your time with the kids and the other leaders." She lifted her eyebrows.

Lilting her voice into a teasing suggestion, clearly,

she meant Evan. No doubt, she and Louanne had gossiped about the arrangements and kept fingers crossed for a budding relationship. "I will." Jayne ignored the innuendo. On the surface, she wouldn't give Mom the satisfaction of a reaction. Inside, anticipation whooshed her stomach over a waterfall, and an unfamiliar surge of excitement splashed over her limbs. But why? Was Evan responsible? For sure, the weekend promised adventure.

At 3:45 p.m., among a growing group of teens, she paced in front of the rec center. Crisp leaves whisked across the sidewalk and blew against the building's sage-green siding. She smiled at the action, acclimatizing herself to the buzz of laughter and energy floating into the neighborhood. She wouldn't relax much this weekend.

"Hi, Jaynie." Louanne tapped her shoulder. "I told your mom I'd chaperone you." She giggled and nudged her arm. She wore coordinating, pink pants and a rose sweater under a mauve, down-filled jacket. A matching visor and knit gloves added a finishing touch. Already, a hint of dusk deepened the blue sky, so the visor was unnecessary. But clearly, she liked the accessory. No doubt, she had packed a color-coordinated hat, in case the weather cooled.

Louanne's promise wasn't entirely a joke. She had always watched over all the kids in town and didn't hesitate to report any misstep to their parents. Jayne forced a little laugh. "Okay, I'll behave."

"If I notice anything amiss, I'll let you know, Louanne." Hands in pockets, Evan appeared, planted his feet apart, and shifted his weight from side to side.

Jayne stepped back and allowed him a close-mouthed smile. A strange, fluttery sensation leapt from her stomach to her chest. With all her legitimate reservations, she should not feel this way around Evan. Did she forget to pack her usual common sense?

Louanne tilted her head, and her visor shielded her eyes. "Oh, Evan, you're such a tease. She's a good girl...most of the time."

Jayne froze. Louanne probably didn't intend her comment to be mean, but her veiled reference to Jayne's life-changing mistake stung. "I'll show you both my model behavior this weekend. Don't worry. I'll keep the kids and the other chaperones in line, too."

"I believe you'll manage the kids okay. You might struggle with the chaperones." Chuckling, Evan raised his eyebrows.

"Where's Dudley?" Always the animal caregiver, Jayne couldn't resist inquiring after Evan's dog.

"Mallory and Cara offered to dog sit. He'll probably gain a couple of pounds with all the treats he'll score. Did Sally stay home, too?"

"She'd chase too many squirrels. I left her with my parents."

"Good choice." He flashed a thumbs-up. "I better help Brad." He strolled away.

"Dr. Scott is a very nice man, and he's even single." Louanne smiled wide enough to show her precise teeth and crinkled her eyes under her visor.

Jayne didn't like the teasing, singsong tone of Louanne's voice. "I'm sure he's a good guy. Will you excuse me, please? I want to say hello to some of the kids." She hustled away before Louanne answered. She didn't disagree but knew a nice man didn't necessarily mean a suitable partner, especially under the circumstances.

Evan skirted the vibrating group of youth.

Jayne headed the opposite way. Still, she glanced over her shoulder and let her gaze linger a second on his back. He wasn't exactly built like a male model—actually, far from it—but he strolled with a likeable, relaxed posture and wore faded jeans, blue sweater, and casual jacket that suited him. A wave of attraction stirred in her stomach. How irrational and inconvenient! Why him? More puzzling, why now?

"Hey, girl. Want a ride?" Tasha hollered out the window, wheeled across the road, and parked on the wrong side, in front of the rec center. "Let's load."

Her son and daughter tumbled out of the van and scrambled to meet their friends.

They'd probably rather ride with Brad than with their mom.

Brad raised a hand and whistled. "Ten in my van. Ten in Tasha's van."

The kids divided into two groups and spilled into the vans.

Jayne braced for the din. The loud, boisterous atmosphere foreshadowed a lively weekend, but she didn't mind. Her work with the youth was rewarding and almost as fulfilling as finding the right home for an abandoned puppy. Stationed by the door, she counted heads and slid her gaze to the back of the van.

At the rear, Evan tossed in assorted gym bags, backpacks, and small suitcases.

The weekend took on a whole new dimension with the rookie chaperone.

Evan slammed shut the back door and rounded the van to the side. "No problem. Take the front."

Jayne halted with one foot on the sideboard and swivelled in time to catch his annoying grin. She had just assumed she'd serve as the copilot next to Tasha, but maybe she shouldn't have claimed the seat. Should she laugh or scowl? He couldn't resist teasing, and she barely stifled her amused reaction. Stiffening, she hopped into place. "Thanks, I will." She buckled her seatbelt. "Newbies in the back." Twisting, she peeked over her seat.

Settled behind Tasha, he grinned and flashed a thumbs-up.

Jayne shook her head. How could a guy irritate yet intrigue her so much?

"Tasha's shuttle service…now departing for Valley Camp." She jerked the van into Drive.

The kids cheered.

Evan tapped the back of Tasha's seat. "How long until we get there, Mom?"

"Sit still. Be quiet back there." Laughing, Tasha crunched over gravel and followed Brad's vehicle to the highway.

"Okay, team. Let's review the plan for the weekend." Jayne glanced from Tasha to the backseat and fixed on Evan's bright face.

He jumped his gaze away from the fields out the window and widened his eyes.

"Brief away, Miss Chief Chaperone." He leaned forward.

"Thank you for showing me the respect I deserve." Jayne concealed her smile and opened the notes on her phone. The hum of tires on the road combined with the teens' chatter filled her head.

"Louanne planned a wiener roast for supper. I'll

organize a game, then you lead tonight's campfire program, Tasha." Familiar excitement sparked at the big weekend ahead. The kids would take home memories to last a lifetime.

"Evan, you're in charge of random fun." She noted his name wasn't on the official list for tonight and couldn't resist teasing. No sense being too serious in his company, and maybe if she showed him her fun side, she'd spare his trying so hard to make her laugh. On the other hand, his chuckle at her comment fanned an ember of satisfaction inside her middle until it spread into a warm glow.

"Fun's my specialty. Bring it on." He laughed and pumped his fists in the air.

"Tomorrow, you don't get off so easy. Brad will handle the morning kickoff, you lead the morning games, and Tasha and I will help wherever needed. Louanne will cook and serve food. I'll lead the sing-along."

"Sounds like a great time, girl." Tasha slapped the steering wheel with one hand.

Jayne stared out the window at the gold fields fading to brown with the remnants of the fall, grain harvest. She hoped camp would be as big a success as Tasha predicted.

In the back, kids laughed, chatted, and shrieked.

She squeezed the armrest. Definitely, with Evan along for the ride, the weekend would be different than the typical youth retreat.

****

Forty-five minutes later, Evan hopped out of the van and surveyed the camp surroundings. He took a deep breath and drew in the scent of clean air laced with autumn nature.

A low, wooden building, likely the lounge and dining area, rested in the middle of a clearing surrounded by tall trees and thick bushes. Most of the branches hung bare. Small cabins nestled in the trees in a semi-circle behind the main building. He'd sleep in one of the cabins with a few of the kids. To the left, in another clearing, a pit ringed with rocks waited ready for a bonfire. Weathered benches and low bleachers surrounded it. Beyond stretched an open patch of lawn where the outdoor games would take place. He liked the layout of his home away from home for the weekend. Evan tromped through crunchy leaves to the back of the van and opened the door to the luggage.

"Grab your bags and head into the retreat center." Jayne waved the teens toward the building.

"Step one, complete." Tasha bounced out of the van and joined Evan and Jayne at the back. Shivering, she zipped her jacket.

"I'll follow your lead, ladies. This experience is all new." Evan stood with hands in pockets, nodded, and smiled at the kids. By the end of the weekend, he'd call them all by name. Right now, they were a blur of blue jeans, fall jackets, bouncing ponytails, and eager faces. Most of the kids knew where to head. He waited until the van emptied and shut the doors.

"Don't worry, brother. We'll show you the ropes." Tasha grinned. "At this point, I cross my fingers for safety and sanity."

"Not to mention buckets of energy and patience." Jayne stretched her lips wide.

Did she bite the insides of her cheeks to prevent a smile from bursting onto her face? Why didn't she just

123

let loose and show her teeth? Clearly, the appearance of her teeth bothered her mother. Jayne's embarrassment at Iris's insensitive comments prickled his neck. Already, she was pretty enough in a quiet way, but he envisioned her face relaxed and bright with gently curved lips and white teeth peeking out. A little crisscross at the front tips only made her interesting and unique.

"Thanks for the warning." He flashed back to the grocery shopping expedition. He'd had more fun tagging along with her, changing a tire, and racing around the store than he'd experienced in a long time— even more than their impromptu lunch date because she actually joked a couple of times. Maybe, sometime soon, she would accept his dinner invitation.

"Just wait." Jayne slung her bag over her shoulder and followed the stragglers into the retreat center.

After introductions, ground rules, and an overview of the weekend's agenda, Brad sent everyone to their assigned cabins.

Evan ended up with the top bunk in a crammed cabin with three sets of bunk beds for five teenage boys and him. The walls were rough plywood decorated with the names of former campers scrawled in various shades of colored ink. He switched on a small electric heater, mounted next to the door, to take the chill off the place. Covered in plastic, the mattresses crackled. A few hooks dotted the walls, and the floor creaked with ancient tile. His head filled with the scent of damp wood and warm bodies. He'd deal with a lot of mess and roughhousing and, possibly, not much sleep.

"Hey, guys," Evan scanned the room and waited until everybody quieted. Two boys sprawled on top bunks, and three others jostled around a pile of bags in the center of the room. "I only ask a few things. Have fun. Stay safe. And let me know if you need anything. Oh, yeah, I haven't chaperoned before. Go easy."

The group laughed.

"Now, remind me of your names before we head to the wiener roast." He pointed at the kids.

"Chad."

"Tyler."

"Will."

"Brandon."

"Kaden."

The guys all dressed pretty much the same in their slouchy jeans and dark jackets. He recognized a few. Tyler towered over the others. Brandon was a bit squatty. Will was the gangly redhead he had met at Adopt-a-Dog. Evan would do his best to get acquainted with everybody. He'd learn something unique about each. "Grab a flashlight, in case you need it later. Okay, let's find the food." He backed out of the way of the commotion stirring the heavy air.

The group leapt over sleeping bags and backpacks and charged out the door toward the firepit.

Evan followed the guys outside and shivered in the chilly wind. He zipped his jacket higher, hustled to the circle, and squeezed into a spot on a creaky bleacher between Tyler and Brandon. He was the middle step with his average height between two extremes.

Brad raised a hand to signal for quiet.

After a few seconds, the hubbub tapered to silence.

"Here's the plan." Brad swivelled so the entire semicircle of kids heard. "Grab a roasting stick, cook a hotdog, and go inside the retreat center to add the fixings. You'll find green salad, potato chips, and cold drinks in there, too. Also, Mallory told me to give this warning. Don't poke anyone in the eye with your stick."

Everybody laughed and filed past the unfinished wooden table where Louanne had laid out roasting sticks and fat wieners.

So far, so good. The kids bubbled with positive energy, and the other leaders welcomed his involvement. He felt right at home.

"Move along, brother." Tasha nudged him forward.

"After you, ladies." He stepped back and motioned for Tasha and Jayne to go ahead. "Jump in before I take more than my share." He patted his stomach. "Got to keep my boyish figure."

Jayne slapped a hand to her mouth and laughed. "I think you missed your chance. But you can delude yourself."

"He's a man after my own heart." Tasha tapped a hand on each ample hip.

"Ouch!" Evan exaggerated a mock sad face. He could stand to lose a few pounds, but he didn't worry about his size. Jayne would forgive a less-than-perfect physique, wouldn't she? Food served as a good antidote for loneliness and boredom, and snacks just plain tasted good.

"Don't pout." Jayne glanced over her shoulder. "I can't stand a whiner."

"Hey, it's my party, and I'll whine if I want to." He grinned and sang a few bars, butchering the lyrics of a well-known oldie.

She snapped back her gaze. Eyebrows raised, she shook her head.

He knew exactly how to get a strong reaction.

Tasha giggled. "I can't wait to hear you sing at campfire."

"I can wait...forever." Jayne crinkled her nose.

Her eyes sparkled, and her cheeks shaded pink from the wind. Hair drawn back in a sleek ponytail, she wore blue jeans, hiking boots, and a tan jacket. Casual and outdoorsy, her style blended with the crowd yet grabbed his attention. Would he ever draw her into a tender hug? For an instant, attraction squashed the air from his lungs. How would his lips feel brushing her cheeks, her forehead, and her lips?

Snapping back to reality, he picked up a stick, slid two wieners into place, and found a spot at the edge of the campfire. Heat prickled his cheekbones, and billowing smoke forced him to cough. He sizzled the hotdogs until they were deep brown with streaks of black. Mission accomplished, he headed inside to add condiments, load his plate with side dishes, and join the kids. Inside the main building, he discovered a wide, open space furnished with tan, tweed couches and thin, brown carpet at one end and, at the other, a dining area with round tables, wooden chairs, and linoleum flooring. "Hey, Gavin, Brandon, Tyler. Mind if I join you guys?" He used his foot to reposition a chair at their table.

Mouths jammed, the guys all nodded.

Wearing identical, black hoodies, they looked like a trio of hungry crows. Evan chomped a bite of hotdog and surveyed the buzzing room.

Jayne wove among the tables and sat with a few of the girls.

So far, the females and males didn't mix much. But

even across the room, her presence sparked his senses.

She flashed a brief smile at the girl beside her and raised her hotdog in front of her mouth.

Empathy lurched in his heart. He wanted to massage her shoulders, lean forward, and press his face against her cheek. Maybe if he was lucky, he'd scoop a spot beside her in front of the bonfire. He'd show her, despite his earlier demonstration, he belted tunes pretty much on key. "What do you guys like best about camping?" He yanked his attention back to the hungry teens around him. He studied them to remember a distinguishing characteristic of each.

"Hanging out with friends and playing games," said Brandon.

He was the short, stocky one with brown hair.

"The food and games," said Tyler with his mouth full.

His dark hair was shaved on one side and longer on the other. A few blemishes dotted his cheeks.

"I, uh…it's all good…" Gavin stared at his plate. He adjusted his black-framed glasses.

"Great to hear." Evan set down his hotdog and wiped his lips and chin with a napkin.

Across the room, Jayne conversed with the girls at her table. She nodded, and her ponytail swished from side to side.

He picked up a few chips, squeezed too hard, and crumbled them onto his plate. "I like the food, and I look forward to everything else, too." The guys would never know how much Jayne grabbed his interest. Chewing a bite, he daydreamed. Earlier, Jayne had joked and teased a little. Should he dare hope she liked him? Around her, his fear of rejection faded. His senses sharpened with anticipation. Did she have any idea of her appeal? He needed to help her understand. Even though he'd give the kids top priority this weekend, could he snag her attention in the midst of all the action?

Chapter 11

Before the evening games, Jayne helped Louanne rinse dishes and load the commercial dishwasher in the camp kitchen. If possible, she'd avoid the topic of Evan.

The floor, walls, and appliances appeared clean, but the room wafted a slight musty odor, like the rest of the old building. In contrast, the fresh smell of lemon dish detergent floated over the sink.

In the dining area, the kids goofed off under the watchful supervision of the other chaperones. Laughter sprinkled over excited voices.

"He likes you." Louanne scrunched her face and shoulders.

She acted like she had just shared a delicious secret. For her cook role, Louanne had tied back her hair into a stubby ponytail and covered her colorful casual wear with a large, white apron.

"Who?" Jayne played innocent, but she clenched her teeth. She dropped a handful of knives into the utensil rack with a satisfying clatter. Sometimes, Louanne was so much like Mom, she could be her twin. She didn't mean any harm, but she loved to poke her nose into other people's business. Jayne backed a step out of Louanne's sight and dared roll her eyes at the woman's back.

"I'll help." Evan stuck his head into the kitchen.

"Thanks, but you better make sure those rowdy boys out there don't break anything." Half turning away from the sink, Louanne dangled her hands in the soapy water.

"In a few minutes, I'll start the game." Jayne dried a large bowl. Grateful for the interruption, she sensed by the way Evan's smile dimmed, he was a little disappointed she didn't invite him to stay. She picked up her pace at drying dishes.

"You bet. See you in a few minutes." He disappeared, closing the door behind him.

"See what I mean?" Louanne threw up her hands, flicking water into the air.

How did the woman jump right back to the earlier conversation without missing a beat? Jayne contained another eye roll.

"Evan wants to spend time with you." Louanne plunged her hands back into the sink.

"He offered to help with dishes." Jayne could have kicked herself for allowing Louanne to tease her into a conversation about Evan. She tossed her hair. "Do you mind if I leave the last things for you to dry? I really should steer the kids into a game. The noise level keeps rising."

"Of course not. Go have fun with the kids...and Evan." Hunching, Louanne smiled over her shoulder.

Jayne threw the towel onto the counter and sped out of the kitchen without responding. In the main lounge area, opposite the connected dining space, she clapped three times and called for the group's attention. "Time to play a game to learn more about each other. Form a circle in front of the couches and chairs, and sit on the floor." She spread her arms, palms down, and lowered them to reinforce her instructions. "It's called *Two Truths and a Lie*." She plopped cross-legged onto the carpet.

"Oh, yeah." Chad nodded and smiled, revealing braces on his teeth.

"I know that one." Kelsey ran a hand through her spiky, blonde hair.

"In any order, share two true statements and one that is false. Then we'll guess the right answer and see if you fooled us. To show an example, I'll start." Jayne scanned the circle.

The other leaders sat interspersed among the kids.

Louanne leaned on the kitchen doorframe with her arms crossed.

"Come join us, Louanne." Evan waved her toward the group.

"No, thanks. You kids play. I'll watch." She wandered to a chair close by.

"Ready?" Jayne tucked a stray hair behind her ear. "I used to manage a pet store." She paused. "I love skiing." She glanced around the circle. "I met a real, live prince."

Some of the girls tittered at the reference to a prince.

Jayne waited until the room settled again. "Now, guess which of my statements is not true."

"You like dogs, so I believe you worked in a pet store." Olivia blinked wide, green eyes and tossed her brunette ponytail. She bent her knees, hugged her long, thin legs, and leaned sideways against Tyler's shoulder.

"Even though the mountains are far away, she probably loves skiing. I do." Chad ran a hand through shaggy, black hair, then rested his forearms on his thighs and rocked.

"Nobody in Prairieville has met a real, live prince." Shaking his head, Tyler scoffed. "False." His dark eyes glinted, and he grinned, revealing large, shiny teeth. He slipped an arm around Olivia's back.

"Hey, she met *me*. I'm a prince of a guy." Evan stabbed his thumbs into his chest.

Jayne smirked. She better contain any sarcastic comments within earshot of the kids. "Give up?" She scanned the circle.

"Tell us." A chorus rang out.

"I don't love skiing. In fact, I've never skied." She raised her hands and flipped her palms.

"You met a prince?" Olivia clapped a hand over her mouth.

"I really did." Sticking her lips together, she smiled and nodded. Fooling the group added to the fun. "Prince Alexander of England visited a food project where I volunteered. He didn't ask me to marry him, but he wondered if I peeled carrots in the kitchen."

Evan tipped back his head and laughed.

The rest of the group joined in.

"Who's next?" She proceeded around the circle and learned an assortment of facts. Tyler once ate an entire chocolate cake. Kelsey won a provincial gold medal in tennis. Will earned one hundred percent on a math test. Chad travelled to Australia. Finally, Jayne pointed at Evan and leaned forward. She shouldn't have been so interested, but for some strange reason, she wanted to know more.

"Number one. Even though I'm a doctor, I don't like needles." He counted on his fingers. "Number two. I have visited every province and territory in Canada.

Number three. I'm adopted."

Jayne swallowed a gasp. A knot of surprise and wariness looped in her stomach. If he truly was adopted, how did he feel about the arrangement? Did he know his birth parents? What were the circumstances?

Kids shouted out guesses.

Evan's statements made her wonder. She held her breath, waiting to find out which was false. If number three was true, would she feel closer to him? When he heard the truth about her and Cara, how would he feel? Her mouth dried, and she swallowed.

"Good guesses." Scanning the group, he nodded. "Believe it or not, number one is true. I don't like getting shots at all. Number two is false. I still haven't visited Newfoundland or Labrador."

So he *was* adopted. Suddenly, the floor felt cold and hard beneath her, and she had the urge to stand, stretch her legs, bolt to the kitchen, and hide. She swept her gaze around the circle of teens and behind, to the wooden walls, tweedy sofas, and group photos. She should take comfort in the rustic surroundings and warm atmosphere, but she shivered.

"I'll tend to the fire." Brad rose and strode to the door.

She nodded and motioned for the next person. Right now, Evan's adoptee status should just serve as an interesting tidbit—no bigger or smaller than anything anyone else revealed. She needed to focus on the kids. Later, she'd find out how he viewed his biological mother.

Often adoptees felt the pain of abandonment, even when they grew up in a loving and supportive adoptive family. Chilled with uncertainty, she hugged her arms around her middle. Would her loving choice and her ongoing involvement prevent Cara from ever suffering those feelings?

"Okay, next. Let's hear from you, Kaden." Hard as she tried to concentrate, she barely heard his facts.

Fortunately, the rest of the group shouted so many answers they likely didn't notice her silence. "Thank you, Kaden." She placed her palms together and rested her hands against her lips in a reflective pose. "I had no idea you were a barrel racer. Now, Olivia's turn."

She stared at Olivia's bouncing, brunette ponytail, but her thoughts leapt back to Evan. Why did she care so much how he felt? How come she felt both drawn to him and a little afraid? Over the years, he had matured and now, he sought friendship...or more. Could she dream of possibilities? Too many things stood in the way, including the threat to her Adopt-a-Dog expansion plans. "Wow, Olivia. Not many people run a half marathon. Let's hear from Brandon."

He flushed pale pink, the color of lemonade, and launched into his truths and lie. Glancing down, he shoved his hands into the pouch of his hoodie.

Jayne took a deep breath. The aroma of burning wood seeped through the leaky windows and nestled in her chest. The scents and sounds comforted her like a warm hug from someone she loved. "Excellent facts, everyone. Most of you really fooled us." She rose from the floor and dusted off the back of her jeans. "Now, let's go outside."

The teens leapt to their feel and jostled out the door.

Through the opening, a distinct trail of smoke wound into the room.

Evan hung back and wandered over to Jayne and Tasha.

"So the doctor hates shots." Tasha laughed and gave Evan a playful punch on his upper arm.

He exaggerated a wince. "You're an award-winning tap dancer?" He widened his eyes at Tasha.

She thrust out her arms, shuffled her boots, swiped toe to heel, and hopped. "You betcha."

Jayne stretched her lips into what she hoped appeared to be a polite smile. Tasha and Evan both had such an easy way with people she envied them. "Let's go join the kids." She led the way.

Outside, the October air nipped her nose and ears, and she squeezed onto the end of a bench. She hugged her jacket closed and joined in the lively songs and crazy actions.

Brandon strummed on a guitar, accompanying them.

The fire crackled, wood snapped, and tall, orange-and-yellow flames leapt into the night sky. Scanning the circle around the sizzling center, she drank in the glowing faces. These teens were lucky to have each other, solid homes, and strong role models in the leaders. If all the pieces worked together, these young men and women would stay on a positive path. She hunched her shoulders against the cold and the past that haunted her.

"Let's close now with an inspiring thought, and afterward, we'll dive into hot chocolate and cookies." Brad wrapped up the program.

"Woohoo."

"Yes!"

The kids cheered the news of more food.

Within seconds, the bleachers cleared, and Jayne found herself seated alone.

Then Evan slid in beside her.

Straightening, she stared at the dwindling fire. Now what? The atmosphere felt too intimate for a casual conversation. She contained a shiver.

"Might as well avoid the rush." Evan rubbed his gloved hands together. "Feels like winter's coming."

"I agree." The weather was a safe topic. If she avoided anything too personal, she'd feel more comfortable. But she couldn't delay forever. She should tell Evan about Cara. Maybe someone had already whispered the details. She could let the rumor mill do its work, but that approach just didn't seem right. He continued to seek her company. She owned her mistake and her decision, and she wanted him to know exactly who he pursued. "Evan..." Jayne squinted at the embers glowing through white ashes and blackened wood. She folded her arms. Embarrassment choked her words. "I need to tell you something..."

****

Jayne's voice nearly blew away in the gusty wind.

"I hope I'm not in trouble." Jayne sounded serious, but Evan threw out a comment to lighten the mood.

"Ha. Not yet."

He studied the wood crumbling into ash and breathed the lingering smoke. The air hung heavy with the sharp scents of autumn. He didn't face her, sensing she almost wanted to be alone.

She stared at the flecks of orange dying in the firepit.

Her face nearly faded into the night.

She hugged her arms around her middle. "You

mentioned you're adopted…"

"All my life." He forced a chuckle. If he hadn't shared his background, he would have avoided questions and comments. But talking openly helped his own healing. Now, what struck Jayne as so important she lingered in the cold to talk?

"I…uh…give you credit for sharing personal details." She glanced over.

Her voice lowered to a near whisper. He shifted on the bench, hunched his shoulders, and tucked his hands under his thighs. The breeze blew in chilly gusts, a foretaste of the bitter weather to come. "I don't hide the fact I'm adopted." He inhaled but couldn't fill his lungs.

Jayne tilted her head and waited.

"When I was seventeen, I contacted my birth mother, but she still wanted nothing to do with me. I was crushed. Finally, when I was in medical school, I received a call. She wanted to meet. By then, she didn't deserve a place in my life. I refused her invitation." He shrugged and shook his head. "I struggle to understand or respect her choices."

Did Jayne inhale a sharp breath, or was the sound just a hiss from the dying fire? Regret climbed into his throat and squeezed the air out of his voice. Wonderful as he found his adoptive parents, how many times had he wished his birth mother had wanted him? Too many to count. By now, the persistent pain had faded to a nagging ache, but it would never totally disappear.

"I'm sorry to hear you suffered and…found the situation…tough…"

"Hey, I survived." He brightened his tone and waited for her to continue. "You wanted to tell me something?"

She shook her head and shivered. "Never mind. It was nothing. We better douse the fire, then grab hot chocolate and cookies before the kids devour all the food." She leapt from the bench, hoisted one of the nearby buckets somebody had filled earlier, and tossed water onto the embers.

Evan finished the job with a second bucketful.

Her tone turned businesslike. Following her into the retreat center, he felt both closer and more distant.

Inside, she scooted away to circulate around the room.

Still curious, he loaded a napkin with cookies and joined a table of giggling teens. What made her change her mind? Would she open up later?

****

The next morning, Evan sat next to Gavin and tipped back a cup of hot coffee. The bitter liquid slipped down his throat and warmed his stomach. He crunched a piece of toast coated in peanut butter and brushed crisp crumbs off his lips. The smell of frying bacon and eggs blasted from the kitchen and tempted him to line up for a second helping. "Having fun so far?"

Gavin swallowed a gulp of orange juice and nodded. "Yeah, camp is cool. I come every year."

His blond hair curled in random directions. Evan could relate.

A few other guys filled the table, joking and laughing between monstrous bites of savory food. The noise in the dining room reverberated off the walls and mingled among the tables with a life of its own. Evan traced Jayne's pathway. Even if his table wasn't full already, he figured she would stick with the girls and avoid him.

"Good morning." Her posture stiff, she held a tray with both hands and glanced down. Her hair swept back into a straight ponytail, and she wore a thick, caramel-colored sweater, fitted blue jeans, and short, brown boots. In her outdoorsy outfit, she could be headed to a riding stable for a morning ride. His gaze lingered, and a mix of compassion and attraction crowded into his stomach.

"Cool you're adopted."

Gavin's quiet voice dragged Evan's attention back.

"Yeah?" Evan waited for him to continue. Hearing the intensity in the teen's tone, he suspected the reason.

"Yeah. I'm, uh, not adopted, but I live with my grandparents." He scratched the back of his neck. "My mom is...she has a drug problem. When I was pretty young, I, uh, lost my dad. He took off."

"Oh, thanks for sharing. How does that arrangement work?" Evan cleared his throat. Gavin appeared to be a normal, well-adjusted kid. People could never tell from the surface what pain and secrets might lie inside. He gulped a deep swallow of coffee.

Gavin shrugged. "It's okay. I'm used to things. My grandparents are pretty cool. They're not old or anything."

"Good. I'm glad. My adoptive mom and dad always treated me well." An empty spot throbbed in his chest where his birth mother's love belonged. "Even though you don't live with your mom, you're lucky you know about her." Why did he make that comment? His feelings were complicated. Even though he missed the affection, he didn't want to know his birth mother anymore. After the way she had rejected him, she didn't deserve a place in his heart. Thankfully, Gavin didn't seek any advice. He probably just wanted to connect with the new leader. "If you ever want to talk about anything, let me know."

"Yeah, sure." Gavin swooped a piece of buttery toast through an egg yolk. "Will you play games today?"

"You bet. Wouldn't miss the fun." He slapped the table with a palm. In an instant, the poignant moment ended. Evan stabbed a large bite of egg, glanced over to the next table, and locked on Jayne's profile. He fixed his gaze on her pointy chin. It moved steadily up and down while she chewed a bite of bacon, He had lain awake for hours last night—not because of the smell of stinky socks in a cabin full of guys, or the muffled laughter continuing way too late, or the sound of wind creaking the wooden walls. He had stared at the ceiling and replayed his conversation at the end of the campfire.

Now, the morning clatter of the dining room dragged him back from his moment of reflection. He finished the last of his breakfast, carried his tray to the drop-off counter, and then headed for the lounge area for announcements.

"How was the first night?" Brad approached from behind and bumped Evan's arm.

"Pretty good. Actually, fun." Evan scanned the room. "Watching the guys awkwardly try to impress the girls throws me back a few years."

"What do you mean transports you back a few years?" Brad laughed and stuck his hands in his front pockets. "Aren't you *still* awkwardly trying to impress a girl?" He tipped his head toward Jayne.

She perched on the arm of a chair and leaned to talk to the girl seated below.

From this angle, he only saw the tip of her nose. "Are my motives that obvious?" Evan chuckled and continued toward a spot on the tweedy couch. Brad knew him well. He snapped his gaze to his business partner's smirk. He didn't mind the teasing. "I'm glad I came. For a lot of reasons." He grinned and flicked his eyebrows.

"Great. Seriously, I'm glad you joined the fun." Brad strode to the center of the room, lifted a hand, and waited for the chatter to quiet.

The room heated almost instantly with all the bodies filling the sofas and spilling onto the floor. Evan welcomed the coziness, in contrast to the chill outside and the empty space inside his heart. What would today bring? Would Jayne broach the mystery topic?

Louanne clutched a dish towel and rested her back against a wall.

Tasha planted hands on hips.

She acted like a teacher ready to pounce on anybody who misbehaved.

Jayne barely caught his gaze and swivelled to face Brad.

The fleeting eye contact caused extra heartbeats to thump in his chest. He couldn't let his reactions continue to intensify. He didn't even know if she liked him.

Why did he land in Prairieville as Jayne's adversary over the much sought-after parcel of land? How could he connect with her on a deeper level? Last evening, she almost confided something. Why did she change her mind? He'd give anything to listen to whatever she wanted to share. He couldn't sort out his confusion in a roomful of noisy kids, but he knew one thing. Jayne hid something important, and he'd find out what.

Chapter 12

Next to Tasha, Jayne circled the playing field. With her down jacket, knit hat, and thick mitts, she dressed to keep cozy outside on a crisp, fall day. The sun shone, and she felt light and optimistic in the peaceful surroundings.

"Evan shows a knack with the kids." Tasha tipped her head in his direction.

"I guess so." Jayne scanned the field and spotted him laughing with a group.

Brad paced the sidelines in his role as referee.

At the moment, the guys didn't need any help with the game. "Let's walk that trail for a few minutes and then check back." Jayne pointed ahead toward a narrow clearing in the trees.

The wind rustled loose leaves along the open field and chased them to the pathway in streaks of gold, orange, brown, and dashes of red. Overhead, Canada geese formed a *V* for the long flight south, and fluffy clouds hung on the blue canopy. Autumn in Saskatchewan was a beautiful time of year.

"You seem a little standoffish with Evan." Tasha touched a hand to Jayne's elbow.

"No, I'm not." Jayne avoided a tree branch.

"I know you, girl, and I recognize standoffish when I see it." Tasha dropped her hand and tromped along at Jayne's quick pace. "What's up?"

"Nothing's *up*. I just don't want to give him the idea that I want to date him or anything." Jayne kicked a small pile of yellow leaves at the edge of the path.

"Why not?" Tasha grinned and gave her a playful punch on the shoulder.

"Hey." Jayne leapt aside. The sight of Evan, bundled in a navy-blue jacket and royal-blue hat when she passed him on the field, and now, hearing his name sent a nervous flutter up her spine. "What do you mean? My hands are full without a guy in the mix. Besides, I count too many reasons a relationship would never work."

"Oh? Name one," said Tasha.

"I'm busy with...my life." Jayne rustled along, and a twig snapped under her feet. "He sits on the wrong side of the land issue. If he and Brad win, I lose. If I win, he loses. Conflict does not bode well for a future together. There. I just listed two good reasons." She avoided two other issues—differing views on adoption and lingering resentment over the university scholarship. Secrets and confusion stirred in her middle. Tasha didn't need to know everything.

"*Your* idea of good and *my* idea of good are not the same, girl." Tasha batted a branch.

Trudging along, Jayne felt her cheeks cool in the wind gusts. Soon they'd glow like a pair of rosy apples. "We better turn around and head back, in case the guys need us." She spun, hoping to leave the topic behind.

"You're not wiggling out of this conversation that easily, girl." Tasha charged to catch up. "Keep listing until you dream up a solid reason."

"He...a couple of things happened in high school that I resent." She whooshed out a breath. Uncertainty

145

scrambled into her chest.

"What? You hold a grudge from fifteen years ago?" Tasha threw up her hands.

"Maybe." Jayne ducked to avoid a pointy branch overhanging the path.

"Dwelling on ancient history makes a lot of sense."

Tasha coated her words with gentle sarcasm.

"I guess you've never heard the expression *forgive and forget*?'"

"And…" Jayne continued like she hadn't heard Tasha. Her friend dared to probe and prod where she should leave well enough alone.

"You heard him last evening. He's adopted." She strode faster toward the clearing ahead. Out in the open, she would escape Tasha's company. She loved her friend, but sometimes, she was a little too outspoken for her own good, or, at least, for Jayne's taste.

"He's adopted. So what?" Tasha raced to catch up. "That situation just gives you something in common, except you've dealt with different sides."

"He doesn't think well of his biological mother." She inhaled the clean, mossy air and exhaled to calm her racing heart. She didn't want Evan to disapprove of her choice. Any hint of reproach would sting as much as her mother's frequent criticism and would forever squelch any hope of friendship, let alone a relationship. She'd rather avoid the shame. After giving Cara the secure home a girl deserved, she worked hard to remain a positive force in her life.

"Why don't you ask?" Tasha puffed. "Whoa, slow down." She tugged Jayne's sleeve. "At that pace, you'll kill me."

Jayne took pity and slowed a smidgeon. She

couldn't possibly ask and risk being judged. She fully intended to explain her close ties with Brad, Mallory, and Cara, but last evening, the words stuck in her throat. "No way. I won't pry into his feelings about his situation or mine. My choice is my business. Now, can we *please* talk about something else?"

"Never say never." Swinging her arms, Tasha laughed. "But just to humor you, what do you think Louanne cooked for lunch?"

"A surprise. I'm hungry already." Jayne scooted ahead. She needed to avoid scrutiny. Tasha meant well, but her unfiltered conversation soaked up energy like a sponge. This weekend had promised a break from everything. A friend should choose a better time—maybe back home—to ask such personal, challenging questions. Her uncomfortable and confused feelings combined into something close to an ache. She felt more like one of the teens out on the playing field than a grown woman. "I'll leave you here to cheer on the kids, and I'll see if Louanne needs any help in the kitchen."

"You can't avoid me, girl." Tasha waved her away. "I know where to find you." She laughed and scrunched her face.

"See you later." She hustled away but couldn't leave the nagging conversation behind. Was Tasha right? Should she talk to Evan about his feelings? Wading into those murky waters might just lead to more anxiety. What if he thought less of her for giving up Cara? He might want nothing to do with her, and she couldn't handle more hurt. Just as unsettling, she saw no obvious solution to the competition over land. He'd already told her he moved to Prairieville because of the opportunities with Brad's clinic.

She stomped her boots clean on the wide steps of the retreat center and braced herself for a few minutes with Louanne. She had escaped Tasha, but she expected Louanne would mention Evan, too. Swinging open the door, she breathed the comforting aroma of fresh bread and spicy chili, a hearty meal for a hungry bunch of teens and leaders. "How can I help?" She poked her head into the kitchen.

Wearing an apron over a magenta sweat suit, Louanne bustled around the kitchen. She stirred a simmering potful of meaty sauce, checked buns in the oven, and tossed coleslaw.

Jayne breathed a sigh of relief. Louanne appeared far too busy to engage in random conversation or teasing.

"Thanks for the offer." Louanne wiped her forehead with the back of her hand. "Please, set out serving utensils, cutlery, and napkins on the buffet table. Then cut the brownies in the big pans over there." She gestured with her head to a wide counter.

"Sure thing." Jayne slipped off her outerwear, washed her hands, and got busy. She did her best to focus on the job and the purpose of the weekend, but the routine tasks left too much time to daydream. Evan offered a lot of strengths. He was attractive enough but not intimidating. She didn't aspire to ever have a partner so handsome he belonged on a magazine cover. He had matured into a nice guy. He was smart and made her laugh. But those qualities didn't make him a prospective partner. Too many other issues blocked the way. How could she even contemplate falling in love with an adversary—especially, a guy who harbored unresolved feelings about adoption? She set down the salt and pepper shakers and surveyed the tables. How could she douse the sparks of interest smouldering in her chest?

Just then, the door banged open, and a trail of kids blew inside, along with a blast of crisp air.

She returned to the kitchen to help Louanne serve heaps of food.

"Quiet, please." Glancing around the group, Brad raised a hand. "Did you like the morning?"

A burst of applause filled the room.

"Good to hear. Now, Louanne will direct traffic to the food." Grinning, Brad swept a hand toward the kitchen.

When Tasha arrived, she steered clear of Jayne but made eye contact, clamped her lips together, and ran a finger along the seam.

Secrets safe, Jayne allowed her a tight-lipped smile and chatted with the kids shuffling along the food line. She'd take Tasha's signal as a promise of no further discussion—at least, during lunch. Of course, her silence wouldn't last for long, but she would enjoy it while she could.

The leaders waited until all the kids dished their food.

Again, Evan waved her ahead. "Just leave some for me."

Noisy chatter bounced off the walls and filled the room with positive energy.

"I might, but no guarantees." She selected a plate. "I can't resist Louanne's cooking." With her tray loaded, she paused and scanned the room for a free spot. One table waited completely open, so she wound over, lowered her tray, and slid into a seat.

Right behind, Evan nabbed the chair beside her. "Mind if I join you?"

"What if I said yes?" She glanced over and raised her eyebrows. Her face felt as hot as when she faced the bonfire. He smelled wonderfully fresh and outdoorsy and even a bit like clean laundry. If she hugged him, she might never let go. Cheeks burning, she buttered a bun. Why did she tease? For sure, he would follow suit. Should she just relax and embrace the fun? Were they more compatible than she admitted?

"Too late." He fingered his utensils. "You're trapped. Today's your lucky day."

"Maybe it's *your* lucky day." She bit into the bun and, when the others joined their table, glanced up.

"I hope so." He grinned and stirred his steaming chili.

"What do you hope?" Louanne took a break from kitchen duty to join the group.

"This food is delicious, and I *hope* you baked us a good dessert, too." Poising his fork, Evan flashed a wide smile.

"Oh, I think you'll be pleased." Louanne clasped her hands and hunched her shoulders.

"I'll save room." Evan glanced around the table. "I can't wait. You must be one of the best cooks in Prairieville."

"Oh, you're very kind…" Smiling, Louanne tilted her head. "Isn't he sweet?"

Staring at her plate, Jayne rearranged her food. She wasn't sure if she would go so far as to call Evan sweet, especially in front of Louanne and Tasha, but she did admire his skilled diversion tactic. She savored a spicy mouthful and nearly relaxed.

"Jayne and Evan, consider this request." Brad paused with his spoon partway to his mouth.

She glanced up, stopped chewing, and sensed Evan in the same pose.

"I need someone to perform a skit this evening." Brad set down his spoon and wiped his mouth. "Will you handle the honors?"

"Oh, please. You'll look so cute together." Louanne beamed and made a faint clapping noise with her fingertips.

Jayne swallowed and opened her mouth to beg off. She squeezed her fist tight until the bun in her hand squished into a lopsided lump.

"You bet." Evan jumped in. "I'll do my best to act as cute as Jayne."

Jayne jerked back her head and widened her eyes. If she laughed at his quip—even if tempted—she'd only encourage more.

****

Evan chuckled at her reaction. For a second, he worried she might choke on her bite of coleslaw. He didn't mean to put her on the spot, but his acceptance seemed harmless enough.

Jayne sipped her water.

She probably wanted to snap that he shouldn't assume she agreed, but she nodded like a good sport.

"Thanks, Evan." She set down her glass and rolled her eyes. "You like to perform. I'd rather watch. Are you sure Tasha can't take my place?"

"Not me, girl." Tasha shook her head and tore open a bun. "He asked *you*."

"You'll be a star." Evan hadn't yet fully endeared

himself, but he'd find a way. "If not, just clap for my performance."

Everyone at the table laughed.

"Thanks for your consolation." Shaking her head, Jayne grimaced.

Her exaggerated reaction assured Evan she wouldn't hold a grudge for long. Maybe she'd even find him fun and want to spend more time together.

Now, after a full afternoon of activities and a lively dinner, he stood in the center of a circle of kids near the bonfire. He basked in their laughter at the simple, slapstick skit. He ad-libbed a clumsy character who fell and flailed around with his nose stuck to the ground.

She played a kind stranger who freed him, then reclaimed her lost chewing gum off the tip of his nose.

The smell of burning wood swirled around, and logs crackled and snapped.

At first, Jayne had delivered her lines like a robot, but she soon loosened up. A couple of times, she flickered a bare hint of a smile, probably wanting to laugh at his antics yet remain in character.

"I liked your actions." Chuckling, Kaden stuffed his hands in the front pockets of his blue jeans.

His freckled face glowed in the firelight and, combined with his small stature, he looked more like an adolescent than a teen.

The rest of the guys echoed his comment, laughed, and jostled each other.

Evan glanced over at Jayne. She interacted with an animated cluster of girls. Judging by her easy giggles and glowing cheeks, she agreed the skit hit the mark and drove an even deeper connection with the kids.

Again, Brad raised a hand. "Time to sing now.

Back to your places."

Everyone returned to their seats for a mix of catchy songs, starting with "Count on Me" about friendship.

Breathing cool, smoky air, Evan clapped along and spotted Jayne across the way.

She clapped and swayed from side to side. The wind blew tendrils of hair across her cheeks.

From his vantage point, the orangey reflection of the fire lit her face and shaded it into a relaxed and peaceful canvas. The minor stress of the performance left no lasting effect.

In a humorous way, the skit had challenged everyone to be kind and think well of others. He checked the kind box. But he didn't think well of certain people. Did he need to change his attitude toward his birth mother? What about Bethany? The questions and answers hurt. He hunched his shoulders and leaned forward to feel more of the fire's comforting heat.

Drinking in the warm atmosphere, he belted out the silly lyrics to "The Quartermaster's Store" and "Boom Chicka Boom." But underneath his jovial exterior, he battled guilt and uncertainty. Could he let go of bad feelings and forgive the things that squashed his chest so hard he could barely breathe? He didn't need to dwell on his absent birth mother or his runaway ex-wife. He could still dream of becoming a father someday. Maybe, he could even attract Jayne. Scanning the group, he caught her gaze.

Sudden optimism inflated his chest like a balloon. He had found the strength to leave Toronto, where bad memories lingered. In Prairieville, he grabbed a new opportunity. Now, he absorbed an atmosphere of kindness and positivity. Inhaling inspiring breaths of autumn air, he clapped and bathed in the glow of the fire.

A bit later, Brad wrapped up the sing-along.

Stretching to shake out kinks from sitting on the hard bench, Evan nodded at the kids drifting by toward the retreat center.

"Coming?" Tyler paused and grinned. "You can tell more jokes."

The teen towered over Evan. He examined Tyler's innocent face, dotted with red blemishes. These kids sought leadership, and he would measure up. Evan gave him a high five. "Go ahead, and in a few minutes, I'll join you. Hey, don't eat all the cookies before I get there."

"Okay." Tyler loped off to catch up with his friends.

Evan's limbs weighed heavy, in a good way, as if he had just awoken from the most restful sleep ever. He had needed this camp weekend more than he knew. Where was Jayne? He floated his gaze along the benches and locked on her back.

She stood with hands in pockets, chatting with Tasha and Olivia.

"Jayne," he called. "Got a minute?"

She spun and spotted him in the flickering light. "I guess so."

He circled to her side of the fire.

She must have told Tasha and Olivia to go ahead, because she was left alone. "Hey, thanks." He faced Jayne. "You made the skit a hit." How could he explain? Would she care that camp taught him a new perspective on his life? He needed to share the good news with somebody. "I learned something, too."

Overhead, the moon and stars glistened, and an owl hooted in the night.

He inhaled the thick air. Why did he choose right now to bare his heart? Should he continue? He couldn't talk long before he'd be missed. Louanne would notice. Tyler waited. His back felt cool compared to his front, facing the dwindling fire.

"Oh, what did you learn?" Hands in pockets, she swayed side to side.

Her question hung waiting for an answer.

"I…" Why hadn't he paused before he acted? Now was not the time to explain. He didn't want to rush the conversation. "I'll tell you some other time." How awkward. Just like Jayne last evening, he couldn't force out the words. Uncertainty raced in his heartbeats.

"Oh, okay." She shivered.

"Cold?" He dared encircle her shoulders with one arm.

"A little." Widening her eyes, she jumped back out of his reach.

"Sorry. Just thought a warm arm might feel good." He should have asked first. "I'm hungry for hot chocolate and cookies. Let's go." He tilted his head toward the retreat center, then paused. "One more thing before we go." His hands quivered in his gloves. "You should smile more."

"Pardon?" Wide-eyed, she snapped her gaze to his face and pursed her lips. "I do smile."

"I mean a real smile." He demonstrated and nodded. "Show your teeth."

She stared at his face and twitched the edges of her lips. She opened and closed her mouth.

"No matter what your mother thinks, your teeth suit you. Let them show." He trailed his gaze from her wide eyes to her mouth and back to her eyes. Did they glisten with moisture?

"I..." She shook her head and crinkled her forehead.

His mouth dried. Maybe he had overstepped his bounds in an offensive way. He punched one hand into the other. "You're attractive—more than you know." Wow. Now, he had really stretched his limits. But Jayne needed to believe she wasn't defective just because of slightly crooked teeth. "Try it."

Slowly, she parted her lips and stretched them into a modest curve that didn't quite conceal her teeth.

"Nice work." Success leapt and slam dunked a basket in his stomach. "Practice. You'll improve. Now let's throw water on the fire and get our snack." She listened. He had convinced her to smile. Now, he couldn't wait to repeat the feat.

Chapter 13

Jayne woke Sunday morning and shivered in the damp, cool cabin. The small electric heater couldn't keep up, and the autumn chill had crept in overnight and draped the room. She snuggled in her sleeping bag for a few precious minutes before she persuaded five teens to start the morning. She was already sorry camp would end at five p.m. today.

On the happy side, she'd return to a wagging Sally and a comfortable bed.

The downside loomed not so inviting. In two days, the town council would meet and decide Adopt-a-Dog's fate. The two weeks since the meeting where they deferred their decision on the parcel of land had zipped by in a blur. With Tasha's enthusiastic help, she had recruited more backing from donors and supporters. But now, she had almost run out of time to sway opinions in the dogs' favor.

A sliver of guilt poked her stomach. She shouldn't think only of the dogs. Stretching, she stared at the knotty ceiling and breathed the woodsy air.

In their own cozy spots, the girls stirred and groaned at the prospect of rising so early.

After she counted down from a hundred, she'd jump out of bed and bundle herself in cozy clothes before the morning chill burrowed into her bones.

Eighty-four, eighty-three... Lying curled in her

thick sleeping bag, she couldn't erase Evan's kind and appealing face from her mind. He had told her to relax her smile and allow her teeth to show. Should she follow his advice? Sometimes, she visualized telling her mom, once and for all, to quit judging her appearance and her past.

She didn't want to straighten her teeth. She widened her mouth, parted her lips, and allowed her upper lip to rise. The foreign sensation felt awkward. Seconds later, she snapped everything back into place, paused, and tested her new smile again. She felt as exposed as stepping naked into a shower. After all the years of concealing her teeth, she'd need to practice the change. She gulped. Why did Evan care how she smiled? Wait. What number had she reached? Having lost count, she shimmied out of the sleeping bag, shivered, and grabbed clothes. "Let's go, girls." She clapped three times. "Rise and shine."

Within a few minutes, everyone rolled out of bed, dressed, and chattered at full volume.

Oh, to be a carefree teenage girl. Jayne surveyed the aftermath of the tornado of activity and closed the cabin door. Later today, at packing time, order would be restored.

Trekking along the pathway to breakfast, Olivia hung back.

Jayne slowed her pace to match. She glanced at the girl's flushed face and slight frown. Her deep-green eyes fluttered. "Do you want to talk?"

"Uh…" She stopped and gazed at the ground littered with leaves.

A flock of geese honked high overhead.

"Go ahead." Jayne resisted the impulse to check

her watch for the time. Breakfast could wait. She waved on the other girls. "See you soon."

"I, uh, wanted to ask you." She hugged her blue down jacket around her waist. "Tyler is my boyfriend, and we, uh, at least, I was wondering if I should go on birth control." Hunching her shoulders, she shifted her feet and crunched a twig. "We haven't, uh, done anything…but you know, uh, just in case?" She glanced at Jayne, then away at the bare bushes behind.

Jayne took a deep breath. Usually, the girls didn't ask such sensitive questions. Was she qualified to answer? She flashed back to her reading and training on communicating with teens. She'd listen without judgment and share perspectives free of pressure. Olivia was only eighteen. What a relief she hadn't made a choice she would regret. Likely, underneath the question about birth control lay the heart of the matter. Olivia struggled to balance the values her parents taught with the reality of life as a teen with a serious boyfriend.

She shivered but didn't want to break the mood by relocating somewhere warmer to continue their conversation. This situation captured exactly why she volunteered her time to lead these young men and women. "I'm proud of you for thinking through your decision." She touched Olivia's arm. "Strong feelings are hard to ignore."

"My mom would say it would be a mistake to…you know…" Olivia glanced up, then back at the ground.

A crow swooped by and cawed.

The sharp call urged her to spill her story. Jayne glanced over her shoulder to make sure no one else overheard. "I'll share my experience."

Olivia lifted her gaze and nodded.

"When I was in my twenties, for a while, I was influenced by the wrong person." Jayne faced Olivia and studied her downturned face. "I wasn't married, but I got pregnant."

Olivia widened her eyes.

Jayne's embarrassment and sorrow crammed in her throat. "I gave up my biological daughter for adoption so she could have a better life than I could give her as a young, single mom." She wouldn't complicate things by explaining her ties to Cara, Brad, and Mallory. The way the four were connected wasn't just her background to reveal. "I still feel the pain of my choices. Of course, my daughter was never a mistake. Everything happens for a reason. She lives in a good home with wonderful parents, so everything worked out okay in the end. But I don't want anyone else to suffer the way I did."

Ducking her chin, Olivia swivelled a toe and crackled leaves. "Thanks. I'll think about everything you said." She glanced up with a hint of a smile. "I won't…you know…do anything."

"I'm so glad." Slowly, Jayne smiled in her new way. "You have a lot of life ahead." She hugged her. "Thank you for reaching out."

Olivia nodded and smiled. "I'm hungry." She straightened and charged toward the retreat center.

"Me, too." Jayne dashed behind, and her stomach rumbled. Maybe she had made a difference, and with any luck, Olivia would choose the right way, as clear as this pathway to breakfast. Within seconds, Jayne entered the retreat center and absorbed a welcome blast of warm air. The sweet aromas of pancakes, butter, and syrup made her mouth water.

"See you later." Olivia scanned the room and chose a table full of girls, instead of a place beside Tyler.

Jayne watched her for a moment, filled a plate, and scanned for a chair. She trusted Olivia wouldn't rush into anything before she was ready. Loud chatter filled the room. Eager to eat, she slid onto a chair at a table occupied by a mix of kids and Evan.

"You're late." Evan grinned across the table and swished a bite of pancake in syrup. "Did you sleep through your alarm? Must be nice, eh, guys?"

"I attended to some important business." She flushed. He could imagine what he wanted about what kept her away. She didn't mind his teasing. She understood—and even liked—his joking style. No one had ever showed such genuine appreciation for her appearance. Nobody else tried so hard to make her laugh. He even liked her teeth. She flickered a smile and imagined a hint of white showing between her lips. Was he impressed? Wait until she asserted herself with her mother.

"Morning, girl." Tasha breezed by with a full tray of used dishes. "You and I lead games this morning." She swung her hips toward the field outside.

"Meet you there." Jayne chewed quickly so she wouldn't hold up the agenda. Thank goodness, Tasha couldn't supervise and matchmake at the same time.

After breakfast, she found the rest of the day flew. She breathed a little easier when, from a distance, she noticed Olivia was curtailing interactions with Tyler.

During a game, he draped an arm over her shoulders.

She ducked away and joined her girlfriends.

Judging by Tyler's stiff posture, he wasn't pleased. Last evening, she had leaned in for a cuddle, but not today. Good for Olivia for rethinking things.

Later, during free time, he motioned toward a hiking trail.

Olivia shook her head and headed in the opposite direction.

Again, Jayne silently cheered. Tough as it must be for Olivia to withdraw and disappoint a nice guy like Tyler, she had just given herself some needed breathing space. Maybe Jayne's humble advice had stuck.

At five p.m., she helped kids load their belongings into the back of the vans for the trip home. She struggled to hold her shoulders level—not because of the weight of the luggage but due to the heavy load that waited at work tomorrow. Only two more days to prepare for the Tuesday evening council meeting, and she wasn't at all ready. The smiling faces of the kids eased her tension a little but couldn't totally buoy her feelings. She slammed the back door harder than needed, and she didn't care. The satisfying force released a burst of frustration.

Evan backed away and raised his eyebrows. "Did I say the wrong thing?" He chuckled and circled to the side door.

"Thanks." Tyler climbed aboard.

"I had a great time."

"I wish we didn't have to leave."

A chorus of voices warmed her heart. The weekend demanded a lot of organization and effort but was worth every ounce of energy. Waiting next to Evan, she high-fived and smiled a little wider than usual. She shuffled sideways to avoid bumping into a girl and accidentally nudged his elbow. An alarming jolt of electricity shot up her arm, and she jumped away.

What just happened? She reacted like her feelings ran deep. But why? She needed to get a grip on her emotions. The situation was too complicated to even contemplate. At best, once all the dust settled from the land issue, maybe she could accept his friendship.

"Hey, I'm not dangerous." Evan raised his palms like he faced a hold up. "You know how to hurt a guy."

She nearly giggled at his exaggerated frown but bit her cheek to avoid flirting. She didn't know how to respond. Last evening, with his warm arm around her shoulders, she had felt the same confusion. Pausing, she searched for a suitably light quip. "A girl can never be too careful." She hopped into the passenger seat and breathed the stale, damp air.

Chuckling, he climbed into the seat behind Tasha.

His joking comment hit home. She'd never intentionally hurt anyone. Still, thinking about the dogs and their welfare, she wanted to lash out at anyone who interfered—including the leaders, Evan and Brad. Her inconsistency twisted into a messy knot in her stomach.

She grabbed the handle and slammed shut the door. The weekend theme reminded her to be kind and think well of others. Forgiving her own mistakes required concentrated effort, too. When she arrived home and took Sally for a long, vigorous walk, she'd sort out the confusing tangle. Right now, she just needed to make sure the weekend ended on a positive note. Evan deserved courtesy, just like everyone else.

"Ready, team?" Tasha turned the ignition. "Buckle up, everybody."

Within an hour, she'd arrive back in Prairieville, and then, as soon as she picked up Sally from Mom and Dad's place, she'd head home to her own sanctuary and remain a safe distance from Evan. Of course, she couldn't avoid encountering him at the council meeting on Tuesday evening and at the youth gatherings on Mondays and Fridays. She'd likely pass him on the street since their workplaces were located so close together. But if he invited her to join him on a walk with the dogs or for a meal at his place, he probably wouldn't like her answer. Separation was the only way she could manage the situation.

****

After work the following Tuesday, Evan tossed his lab coat, decorated with garden tools, into the office laundry bin. Soon, he'd switch to winter themes, but rakes still worked with the number of leaves drifting on lawns and streets. The space was neat and sterile with the scent of antiseptic permeating the entire clinic.

"Did you have a good day?" Brad lathered his hands at one of the sinks near the examination rooms.

"Super." Evan ran water and squirted soap at the adjacent sink. "I like Prairieville. So far, all is well. I just hope for the best at the meeting." Tonight was the all-important session at the town council. Members would decide the path for the clinic. The vote—with any luck—would confirm he made the right choice in relocating here. He shut off the water and dried his hands. Could he drum up an option that would meet the needs of the medical clinic *and* Adopt-a-Dog? That discussion would wait.

"I'll see you there." Brad dried his hands and added the towel to the laundry.

"Sounds good. I foresee an interesting evening." If the council's vote didn't tip in favor of the clinic, the results would force a Plan B. He wouldn't give up his goals, and neither would Jayne. Conflict loomed yet didn't scare him. He'd find a win-win solution. Picturing Jayne's reaction if she was not the successful proponent hit him like a prairie storm. For some reason, her disappointment mattered more than his own. "See you later." Evan raised a hand. "Say hi to Mallory and Cara. Come, Dudley." He snapped off the lights and locked the door.

Outside, he breathed the sharp scents of autumn. All day between patients, he had reflected on Jayne and the youth retreat. They both verged on sharing something important. What did she almost confide? Would she care to hear the insights he gained at camp? He'd circle back to finish those conversations.

Dudley woofed at a skittering leaf.

Tugged back to reality, Evan picked up his pace. "Let's hurry home to feed you, Dud." He rubbed his dog's furry sides. Despite the nickname, his loyal retriever was anything but a dud. "Heel." He flipped up the hood of his jacket against the chilly breeze, rounded a corner, and nearly plowed into Jayne and Sally. "Well, hello." He inhaled a sharp breath. Instantly, he read the lines of tension along her forehead. The meeting loomed like a scary stranger.

"Oh, you startled me." Jayne widened her eyes, then lowered her gaze to the sidewalk. She folded her lips into a firm, straight line.

Her expression closed like a book. Any progress he had made in winning her friendship—or more—over the weekend sprinted away. He floundered for the right

165

words to coax her new, wider smile but could think of none. "See you later."

She paused only long enough to let Sally bump noses and sniff Dudley. "Yeah, see you at the meeting." Underneath her khaki-colored jacket, she stiffened.

He understood the importance of the decision. She cared deeply for the dogs and their well-being. He was the competitor who could enable or shatter her dream. What could he do or say to assure her he meant well and, no matter what the decision, would hold no animosity? "May the best team win," he called to her blurred profile and then her back. "I won't hold any grudges. Don't forget about dinner at my place."

Without breaking stride, she rotated partway and raised an arm in a slight wave.

His heart rate accelerated like a race car. He needed to share his feelings and scoop her into his arms. But would she open her heart to the possibility?

Crisp leaves scuttled across his path. "She's worried about tonight." His dog was a good listener.

Trotting along, Dudley woofed.

Since camp, Evan had changed. But could he actually forgive his birth mother for abandoning him and refusing to participate in his life until too late? After surviving Bethany's painful departure, could he find love again?

At home, he fed Dudley and threw together a quick supper of grilled chicken and steamed vegetables. Already, his place felt familiar and homey. Colors in shades of browns and beiges created a cozy atmosphere, and the fireplace promised to add warmth. The kitchen was plenty big enough to hold a table for four. He had even added a splash of color with blue placemats and matching towels. Not bad for a single guy. Maybe when Jayne saw it, she'd admire his decorating attempts. "I'll leave you at home for a while." He rinsed dishes and gave the dog a vigorous pat. "I don't know how the council feels about pets at their meeting." Dudley's wide, panting mouth suggested he smiled and understood.

One of the joys of small-town life was Evan could walk almost anywhere. Breathing crisp, musky air, he jammed his hands into his jacket pockets and hiked at a brisk pace. He passed tidy homes with lights sending a glow toward the street. Along the way, he linked up with Brad. "Well, how do you feel?" Evan glanced over.

"Not sure." Brad stared ahead down the street toward the Prairieville Town Hall.

Pressure leapt from Evan's stomach to his chest. "Both proposals show merit."

"Jayne fights hard for dogs' rights." Swinging his arms, Brad chuckled.

"No kidding." The situation was not a bit funny. He hated to think about crushing her hopes and causing deep disappointment. "I hear the vote could swing either way." He pictured her downturned expression, crossed arms, and stiff back. He swallowed. Her feelings mattered.

At the door of the town hall, he paused, took a deep breath, and clenched the door handle. "After you." He ushered Brad ahead. Slipping inside, he scanned the hallway and recognized a few patients and townsfolk but didn't spot Jayne. A familiar smell of old wood closed in. Maybe he kept safer from a distance. Her gaze might shoot daggers, and he could dodge them in the oval meeting room better than face-to-face.

Settled next to Brad on the wooden seats, he slid his gaze across the council members spread along the front, then to the gallery filled with interested observers. The green carpet absorbed the murmur of conversations. He spotted Tasha first.

Dressed in vibrant colors, she lifted a hand and beamed a wide smile.

Next to her, Jayne focused her gaze straight ahead onto Mayor Tommy's jovial face.

Nervousness twitched in his stomach. Evan felt slightly ill. Very soon, he would know the outcome of the council's deliberation. He would leap into action with expansion plans.

She wrinkled her forehead and frowned.

The mayor chatted and chortled with his peers.

With his casual approach and rumpled shirt, he could be watching a baseball game. He didn't project the image of someone about to make a significant business decision. Evan glanced at his watch. One minute to go. He was ready.

At exactly seven o'clock, Tommy rapped the gavel three times. "I now call this meeting to order." He paused and chuckled. "The word *order* reminds me of take-out burgers." He rubbed his round stomach. "Let's blow through this agenda. Then I'll give Sam a little business." He rapped again.

A large lump of trepidation landed in Evan's stomach. No doubt, Jayne felt just as nervous and maybe even more so. He inhaled a deep breath. Would the mayor utter the words he hoped to hear?

Chapter 14

Jayne felt Evan's gaze, and it heated her cheeks. She stared ahead at Mayor Tommy. The guy boosted town morale, but he could project a more dignified image. Sitting next to Tasha, she bounced her knees and clasped her hands together.

"You're shaking me, too, girl." Tasha leaned over and whispered, "Try to relax."

Jayne nodded, but she couldn't hold her legs still. Two weeks ago, she had waited in almost this very spot and studied the knots in the wood panelling and the streaks across the worn carpeting. So much had happened in the past fourteen days, the elapsed time felt much longer. Still, the weeks had flown by, and she could have used double the hours to campaign. Shifting her gaze sideways, she widened her eyes.

In the full gallery, to the left, Mom huddled beside Louanne.

Why were they here? They dressed like a pair of cheerleaders in similar sweaters—Mom's in baby blue and Louanne's in soft peach—and wore their hair twisted up into tidy knots. She elbowed Tasha and tipped her head an inch. "Look who's here."

Tasha raised her eyebrows.

Of course, Mom understood the importance of this meeting. She had even made some calls and knocked on a few neighbors' doors to rally support for Adopt-a-

Dog. Afterward, she didn't mince words. "I hope you realize you face stiff competition, Jaynie." She tutted her tongue. "To tell you the truth, dear, I feel a little torn myself. Dogs are important. Your dad and I love Sally, but we need to consider our health, too." She patted her arm. "Some of the older folks would prefer to access more medical services right here in Prairieville. If you aren't the successful bidder, don't be too disappointed."

Jayne had just clamped her mouth. She wouldn't give up yet, no matter how hard anybody tried to prepare her for the worst.

Now, Mom waited to hear the outcome in person.

Jayne glanced over and spotted her scrunching her face into a sympathetic expression.

Mom waved down low by her knees.

The motion reminded Jayne of school concerts where Mom attempted a subtle wave but didn't fool anyone.

Louanne mouthed, *Good luck.*

Jayne acknowledged them with a slight nod and snapped her attention back to Mayor Tommy.

"Good evening, folks." He scanned the crowd. "Nice turnout tonight. You can call me Tommy-on-the-spot for starting right on time." He chuckled and swivelled his chair.

Mild laughter rippled through the crowd.

Jayne contained an eye roll. He should jump to the point and put her out of her misery. Stealing a glance to her right, she spotted Evan.

He glanced over, then toward the front. The burning in her cheeks intensified. Why did Evan produce this alarming effect? She just needed to hear the decision and exit.

"Thanks, everyone, for coming to spend a little quality time with yours truly." Mayor Tommy stabbed a thumb into his chest and laughed so hard his shoulders shook. "Here goes." He scanned left and right at the council members and swept his gaze over the gallery. "You expected to hear a decision tonight. Adopt-a-Dog and the health center both submitted thorough and impressive proposals. They didn't even have help from this load of brains." He tapped his temple. "Over the past two weeks, both groups talked to the community to gather support. Many people phoned, emailed, and met with me. My only complaint is no one brought cookies." Laughing again, he rocked back in his chair.

Jayne wanted to leap forward and shake him. His attempts at humor only irritated her. Why drag out the verdict? She glanced at Mom, hunching next to Louanne.

Elbow propped on a knee, Mom bit her nails.

Jayne peeked to her right toward Evan. Her heart pattered like rain on a roof.

Evan exhaled a breath and lowered his shoulders.

"Don't worry, you *will* hear a decision." Tommy grinned. "Probably *not* the decision you expected." He paused while a groaning murmur travelled around the room. "Can anyone perform a drumroll?"

A balding council member, who liked to joke almost much as Tommy, beat on the desk.

"You expected a vote," said the mayor. "I reviewed the options with my colleagues and decided both proposals show merit. They would add value to Prairieville. The task to choose one over the other was impossible."

Jayne held her breath. Would he just announce the news? She told herself not to glance at her mom, but an invisible rope tugged her gaze there.

Mom leaned forward with crossed fingers.

Even though she meant well, her presence felt more like pressure than support. She wouldn't hesitate to express a strong opinion on the outcome.

Louanne mirrored her pose.

"So, we decided not to choose." The mayor leaned and planted both hands on the desk. "We can't create hard feelings and divide the town. Our decision is…another drumroll, please."

Jayne gulped. What did he mean they decided not to choose? Would he table the proposals again? She held her breath and fisted both hands. How long could the council drag out this painful process?

"Catch, Jayne, Brad, and Evan." Mayor Tommy mimed a baseball toss. "We throw the challenge to Adopt-a-Dog, to the medical clinic, and to the town. You can't both build on the same piece of property, but…where are you?" He scanned the crowd and pointed at Brad and Evan with one hand and Jayne with the other. "The council requests you work together and come up with a win-win solution. If you collaborate, you can both meet your goals."

A buzz travelled over the room like a bumblebee. Jayne wanted to duck to avoid a sting. She had expected to leave this meeting knowing exactly where she stood, but now… She folded her lips together.

"We didn't get a *no*, girl." Tasha patted Jayne's shoulder.

"True…" Had she really expected a win? At least, the verdict offered hope, even if it forced her to work with Evan to find two solutions. Her current proposal was logical, convenient, and worked within the Adopt-a-Dog budget. To deliver on the mayor's request, someone had to change their plans.

Jayne blinked and stared at Mayor Tommy. Disbelief thudded in her chest. Her skin tingled with an entire roomful of gazes jumping between her and the medical duo. Determined to prove she accepted the challenge, she forced her stiff lips into a scant smile. She refused to glance at her mother so she avoided a deep frown or moist eyes. Louanne probably clapped a hand over her mouth. Jayne did not need sympathy. If she detected a pitying, crinkled expression, she might burst into tears.

Jayne definitely couldn't glance right and catch Evan's reaction, in case he flashed a big thumbs-up or some other dramatic sign of celebration. Under a spotlight, she needed to digest the news before she gave an honest reaction. Right now, a ball of uncertainty bounced between her stomach and her heart. A major obstacle blocked her way; yet she could still hope.

Time swirled in slow motion, and she fought to focus on the mayor's instructions. Although she heard the words, she couldn't exactly process their meaning. Images of needy dogs crowded into her mind until it overflowed like the shelter. The dogs were her passion. They relied on her. She was their voice. "What does he mean?" She muttered under her breath to Tasha.

"Darned if I know, girl," Tasha whispered back.

"Have fun." Mayor Tommy spun his chair. "The council will support two proposals, as long as you both end up satisfied. Prairieville is one, big, happy family. The whole town will thank us for two positive changes.

Good luck!" He delivered a gigantic wink to the gallery.

A silent pause hushed the room like new-fallen snow. Then quiet applause began in the middle of the gallery and spread outward until the whole crowd joined.

Palms planted on her lap, Jayne used all her strength to raise her hands and clap. She could win, and so could Evan. Now, in a way, they played on the same team.

"Okay, folks, that's a wrap. I'm anxious to order that burger I mentioned earlier." Mayor Tommy laughed and rubbed his stomach. "On second thought, maybe I'll switch to a chicken wrap." He heaved his rotund body out of his chair. "Here we go." Tasha tapped Jayne's shoulder. "Smile, girl."

The crowd rose and filled the room with laughter and conversation.

Jayne just wanted to escape and think about how to proceed. Unfortunately, she couldn't magically disappear. People milled everywhere and blocked her way.

A few supporters rushed over to offer encouraging words.

With Tasha, Jayne wove into the traffic and headed for the exit, but partway to the door, she felt a tap on her back.

"Excuse me, Jayne."

She spun and faced the sole reporter from the local newspaper. "Hi, Danielle." Wearing blue jeans and a casual jacket, she still dressed like a student, even though she held a journalism degree and boasted several years of media experience. Jayne shouldn't be surprised Danielle wanted to cover the story. Probably, she had expected to report on the direction for the coveted property. Now, the story would discuss how the proponents would work together on a win-win solution.

"Brad referred me to Evan on behalf of the clinic. Can I get a picture of you two together and a quote for the paper?" Danielle licked her lips and brushed back her thick, auburn hair.

Stories in a small-town newspaper weren't exactly investigative reporting, but they kept locals abreast of community developments. Expansions of local facilities interested almost everyone. "Uh." Jayne needed time to collect her thoughts. What could she say that she wanted quoted? What message did she want Prairieville residents to hear? For Evan, words always flowed. Unfortunately, she didn't possess the same gift.

"Of course, you can grab a picture and an interview." Tasha nudged Jayne's elbow and leaned close to her ear. "Any publicity helps." Under her breath, she muttered encouragement.

Nothing fazed Tasha. Jayne loved her, even though she had overstepped the bounds of friendship and co-worker. She shouldn't speak for Jayne. "I guess so." Jayne scanned ahead to spot Evan in the swirl of people. She hadn't planned to interact with him this evening, and now she'd pose beside him for the local paper. Dismay pinched her throat. Would anything unfold as expected?

****

Evan followed Danielle's instructions and waited along a patch of wall to the left of the exit. Hands in pockets, he chatted and laughed with Brad and the town pharmacist. Other medical professionals sided firmly with expanded medical services, which meant good news for him and bad news for Jayne. Would she consider relocating? Uncertainty hardened his chest and shoulders into rocks.

Shooting Tasha a glare, Jayne trailed Danielle.

From Evan's vantage point, he observed all the groupings and dynamics of the crowd.

Jayne's mom beelined for Jayne, with Louanne hot on her heels.

Now, Jayne faced a reporter, her mom, Louanne, and him, all at the same time. Like she did so often, she clamped her lips. He hadn't expected media attention, and judging by Jayne's tense posture, neither had she. Accepting Danielle's presence didn't bother him, but seeing Jayne approach in her fitted jeans and shape-hugging sweater spun an unsettled sensation into his stomach.

"What good news, Jayne!" Mrs. Jones caught up and tugged her arm. "You can still make your wish come true. Maybe not the way you expected, but you never know. Every cloud has a silver lining." She lowered her voice. "Oh, hi, Evan. Don't mind me. I might sound a little biased."

Louanne sneaked in on the other side between Tasha and Jayne. "I'm sure you and Evan will enjoy working together." Covering her mouth, she giggled.

"Hi, Mom. Hi, Louanne." Jayne offered a small, close-lipped smile. "Sorry, I can't visit at the moment. Danielle wants to take my picture."

"Oh, how wonderful!" Jayne's mom clapped. "I'll send a copy to Aunt Patsy and your brother. Your dad will be so proud. I told him he should come to the meeting."

Jayne's face shaded to a deep red, the color of a ripe tomato. Her mom's and Louanne's comments, the buzz of the crowd, and the prospect of appearing in the paper must stress her to an uncomfortable degree. "Hey, Jayne." Evan raised a hand. "The council sure handed us a surprise on a silver platter tonight. Hello, Iris. Hi, Louanne. Long time no see."

"We spent a lovely weekend together, didn't we?" Louanne laughed and placed a hand on Evan's forearm. "Now, you get to work with Jaynie again." She winked and waggled her fingers.

Evan grinned and nodded. Louanne could tease all she wanted. "My lucky day." Poor Jayne. Her nickname sounded even more childish coming from Louanne. She would also hate the innuendo about possible romance.

Danielle motioned for Jayne to stand closer to Evan. "Smile, and pretend you're happy with the decision—or rather, lack of a decision. At least, I assume you feel good. After the picture, I'll jot a quote." She tucked her notepad under an arm and adjusted the camera. "Hey, how about a thumbs-up?"

"Wait, wait, wait." Iris jumped between the camera and Jayne. "A few hairs straggled out of place, Jaynie. Here, let me." She flicked the front and sides.

"Mom, please." Jayne shook her head free, and her hair swayed, no tidier than before. She sighed and glanced from Danielle to Evan.

Evan didn't mind the photo request, but Jayne probably wasn't as keen. He grinned and swooped his thumb forward. He glanced over and sucked in a breath. Her tousled, carefree style was alluring in an outdoorsy way. But when she viewed the picture, what would she think of a few stray hairs? Maybe she should have accepted her mom's help.

"Okay, let's try again. On three." Danielle adjusted her position. "One, two, three."

Jayne barely stuck out her thumb in time, and just as the camera flashed, she glanced at Evan.

At the same instant, he flipped his gaze her way and locked on her wide-eyed expression.

"Nice," Iris commented first. "I almost see a smile."

"What do you mean *almost*?" Louanne brushed a hand on Mom's arm. "What a sweet couple." She giggled and winked.

"Thank you. I got a good shot." Danielle adjusted the camera on her shoulder and grabbed her notepad.

"Hey, gals." Tasha raised her hands. "Let's get a head start and save a table at Sam's. We'll have coffee together."

Smiling, Iris flitted her gaze from Tasha to Louanne and back. "What a nice idea!"

"Oh, yes." Louanne zipped her peach fleece jacket. "I would enjoy herbal tea to finish the evening."

Evan bet Jayne could have hugged Tasha for dragging away her mom and Louanne. He didn't mind who listened. She probably didn't need an audience for Danielle's interview.

"Perfect. See you soon." Shifting, Jayne lifted a hand in a half wave.

Feeling the tension, Evan imagined Jayne nearly rolling her eyes. He breathed easier—not for himself but for her. Compassion and attraction melded in his chest. He cared how she felt, and he believed they could share a future. With her steady presence, she wasn't the type to skip out on a commitment. Judging by her work with youth and her fondness for Cara, she liked children. She was exactly the woman he needed.

Danielle poised her pen. "Jayne, were you surprised at tonight's decision?"

"Uh, yes. I anticipated leaving with a concrete answer about whether to proceed with renovations. Ideally, we will know before winter hits so bad weather doesn't delay construction."

"How do you feel now?" Danielle scribbled on her notepad.

"I'm very happy the council supports both projects." Shifting, Jayne glanced at Evan. "But we need to work out a lot of details. The biggest one, of course, is who gets the original plot of land and who moves elsewhere."

"Thanks, Jayne." Pen poised, Danielle faced Evan. "Now, same questions. Were you surprised?"

"Surprised? Yes. Disappointed? No." Evan shook his head. "I look forward to working with Jayne and the community to find another option for one of the projects. I support a win-win approach. No one loses in this situation. You can count on Jayne and me to compromise. We'll do it sooner than later." Hopefully, he didn't speak out of turn.

"Thank you, Evan. You just answered both my questions." Danielle tapped the pen on her chin. "Hmmm. Is there anything else? Oh, yes, Evan, you arrived here less than a month ago. How well do you know Jayne? At least, why are you so sure you'll work well together?"

Danielle really should focus her questions on the business angle and not the personal side of the story.

Jayne widened her eyes.

What could he say and not embarrass her with his answer? He averted his gaze. "Jayne and I knew each other in high school. She worked hard then, and I suspect her work ethic hasn't changed. Even as I talked to townsfolk about the clinic, I heard lots of comments about how well she manages Adopt-a-Dog. I also just helped chaperone the youth retreat, and I observed how well she connected with the group. She always shows integrity."

Evan swivelled and slipped his hands in his pockets. He didn't add how he trusted her without question. Starting in high school, she had treated him well—*so* well a worm of guilt still crawled inside his stomach. He'd do anything to repair the damage, including offering well-deserved praise. He squirmed at her discomfort. Her cheeks had shone pink before, and now, the color deepened to the color of a bad sunburn.

"Your turn, Jayne. What tells you Evan and you will work out an acceptable plan?"

"I believe his word." Jayne paused.

She stopped short of declaring she trusted him. But *believing* headed in the right direction. He straightened. Hope squared his shoulders.

"He also owns a golden retriever. People who love dogs display caring hearts and understand animals' needs."

"Oh, interesting." Danielle scratched more notes. "Is there anything else either of you would like to add?

"I'll arrange a meeting with Jayne tomorrow. We can't waste time." Anticipation raced his pulse.

"Agreed, Jayne?" Danielle smiled.

"Agreed but…oh, never mind." She dropped her gaze to her hands.

What did Jayne start to say? "This fact is strictly off the record, Danielle." Evan rolled from heel to toe and back. "I'll invite Jayne to discuss details over breakfast at Sam's. We'll keep you updated on our progress."

"I'll hold you to your promise." Danielle closed her notebook. "Good luck."

Jayne widened her eyes and swallowed. She smiled broader than usual.

Quirking an eyebrow, Evan faced her. He caught a glimpse of her white teeth. She had listened to his advice, and the results showed. Admiration jumped into his chest. The change couldn't be easy, but she was determined. "Does breakfast at seven tomorrow morning work?"

Chapter 15

The next morning, Jayne examined her appearance in the full-length mirror in her bedroom to make sure she captured the right mood for a breakfast meeting. The pale, grayish-blue walls normally surrounded her with a soothing backdrop, but today, they didn't work their calming magic. No matter how she felt, between the youth group and the expansion plan, she was forced to connect with Evan.

The flutter inside her intensified much bigger than butterflies. Was it a dragonfly or a hummingbird? She turned her back to the mirror and checked the view over her shoulder. Her dressy jeans showed off her shape, and a crisp, white shirt sent a more businesslike image than her usual work attire. She'd pack old jeans and a hooded sweatshirt to change into at the shelter.

Hesitating, she undid a second button on her shirt. Not too revealing, the open neckline hinted at her femininity. Why did she want to remind Evan? Would he notice? Ready to go, she hugged Sally, smoothed on lip balm, and practiced a full smile. "I'll pick you up at lunchtime, Sal."

A few minutes later, she left behind the autumn chill and stepped into the warmth of Sam's.

Settled in a booth, Evan sipped coffee.

She inhaled the savory aroma of eggs, bacon, and hash browns swirling from the kitchen. A quick scan of the diner confirmed Mom and Louanne weren't here this early. Not that she expected to see them, but she couldn't handle another encounter this soon. She slid into the booth and faced him. Evan had dressed carefully for the occasion, too. His hair spiked with help from hair gel, and he wore a striped dress shirt with navy-blue pants. The wings of anticipation inside her beat a little faster.

"Thanks for joining me." He set down his mug and offered the menu. "The special looks good."

She glanced down but couldn't concentrate on the options. "I'll have the same. Let me place our orders." Weaving between tables toward the front counter, she sensed his gaze burning her back. The sensation made her a little uncomfortable but, at the same time, sent a delicious tingle up her spine. Task complete, she settled into her spot and gazed across the table.

"Last evening, your mom burst with pride." He chuckled and looped a finger through the handle of his coffee mug.

"She shows extreme interest in every aspect of my life. Is she proud?" Jayne shifted her gaze away. "Sometimes." Her teeth and her past didn't rank in the proud category. She wrestled a napkin out of the dispenser on the table.

"Definitely, she loves you. You're lucky." He gulped a steaming mouthful.

"I know. I don't mean to complain. Being unloved would be way worse." She grabbed a wrapped set of cutlery from a ceramic container beside a set of salt and pepper shakers. Why did his expression droop?

The door banged, and a rush of cool air whooshed by.

"Missing out on a parent's love hurts. Believe me." Evan gulped a mouthful of coffee.

His comment fell between them like rain. The jovial Evan covered some deep-seated pain. Watching his rapid blinks as he stared out the window, she resisted an overwhelming, invisible tug. She wanted to listen, hug, and reassure him, but this time together was not an intimate conversation around a campfire. The purpose was serious business.

She lightened the mood with small talk until their food arrived. "Thanks, Sam." She eyed the loaded plate, and her mouth watered. The cozy atmosphere and savory scents helped calm her jittery insides.

"Enjoy." Sam topped up Evan's coffee and placed a full mug in front of Jayne.

"Let's dig into our food and our options." Evan surveyed his plate.

His voice returned to its usual, upbeat tone. He did well at hiding his pain, but it must lurk under the surface.

He lifted a fork and broke the yolks on his eggs. "We will determine the best solution very soon."

Last evening, Evan's glowing commentary on her integrity had filled her with sunshine. Did his praise erase any lingering anger and bitter feelings? Maybe. But her flip-flopping emotions confused and exhausted her. He had proven he respected her and cared. Did she feel the same? How could her feelings become so entangled? "Adopt-a-Dog can't afford a whole new location." Jayne spread raspberry jam on toast. She might as well lay the issues on the table right away.

"Hey, let's brainstorm ideas before we fire challenges." He swished a piece of toast through the egg yolk.

The clatter of dishes and murmur of conversations kept their discussion private from other diners.

"Morning." He raised a hand to a man brushing by the booth.

"Good plan, Mr. Positive." Jayne smiled and let her teeth peek underneath her top lip. He would notice for sure and realize he had already boosted her confidence. Maybe that knowledge was not a good thing. She closed her mouth, then opened it just wide enough to slip in a bite of salty bacon.

"I see several choices." He swiped at his mouth with a napkin. Leaning forward, he rested both forearms on the table. "We stay status quo, which doesn't benefit either project or the community. Or we both relocate elsewhere, which leaves the town with two vacant properties. Or one stays, and the other goes. Did I miss anything?"

He offered a good list but missed one idea worth consideration. "We could talk to the businesses next door and ask if they plan to close or move. If so, we could both remain where we are *and* expand. The possibility is unlikely, but you never know…"

"Aha, good thought." Evan pointed his fork.

She pretended to duck out of the way. "Careful you don't poke out an eye." A flush washed her face. Why did he have this effect? She lifted her coffee mug. Maybe it would cover the evidence his compliment rattled her more than a little.

"Don't worry, I'm a doc. I'll fix any damage." He widened his eyes, laughed, and stabbed a bite. "But I agree. Safety first. Seriously, I like your idea. You know the local businesses better, so would you be willing to approach them? What are they—a florist on your side and a law office on mine?"

"Okay, I'll inquire." She balanced her elbows on the table and used both hands to hold her mug and partially conceal her face. Thank goodness, the heat in her cheeks subsided. "What, may I ask, will you do?"

"I'll scout other locations." He gulped a swallow of coffee.

"For both projects?"

"Honestly, I'll start with Adopt-a-Dog."

She stiffened and narrowed her eyes. "Why not yours?"

"People like the location. The clinic has been situated there for decades." He studied her expression. "Ample parking on the street is very convenient. You probably get less walk-in traffic. A place on the outskirts could work well to give dogs more space to exercise. The rent might be cheaper, too."

Wariness landed in her stomach and squeezed her breakfast. His idea made sense, but she hated to concede. Still, stubbornness didn't belong in a win-win scenario. She paused, took a deep breath, and stared out the window. "Okay."

"We'll report back by the end of next week." He bumped a palm on the table. "Deal?"

"Deal." She couldn't make her voice sound quite as emphatic as his confident tone.

"One more thing, Jayne...or should I say Jaynie?" Chuckling, he draped his napkin across his plate.

"Never." She grimaced, even though his gentle teasing felt good. "Mom and Louanne own that one. Much to my chagrin."

"Next time, can we meet at my place?" Smiling,

Evan raised his eyebrows. "Bring Sally, too. Dudley approves. I already promised you a sample of my gourmet cooking."

Her heart surged. Dinner sounded suspiciously like a date, and she shouldn't tease her heart. She could only be a friend. "A business dinner?"

"A dinner between colleagues and friends. *Good* friends and dog lovers." He raised his eyebrows.

She paused and silently lectured the excitement jostling her heart, but her efforts didn't work at all. His soft eyes and earnest expression melted her resolve, and a surge of attraction raced throughout her body. "I guess so. I'll bring a salad." She might regret her decision, but the words *no, thank you* evaporated from her tongue.

"I better get to work." He maneuvered out of the booth.

"Me, too. Tasha and the menagerie await."

"I'll see you next Saturday at six, if not before. We'll explore options before we report back."

She stood, faced him, and breathed his clean, masculine scent. The din of voices and dishes faded to the background, and the kitchen steam surrounded them in a private cloud.

He extended a hand.

She jerked a sudden step back to resist his magnetic attraction and shook it to seal the deal. His skin felt smooth and firm, and the pleasurable sensation sent warmth up her arm. Time with Evan proved a very unsettling mix of personal, volunteer, and business connections. Steadying her balance, she spun and led him out the door. The chilly blast of air cooled her hot face. She had a lot to research in the next ten days and much to think about before next Saturday evening.

****

Late Saturday afternoon, Evan popped lasagna into the oven and spread a red-and-white tablecloth. He stood back, then rustled in a drawer and added red candles and white napkins. Not bad. Definitely, a touch of romance. Anticipation quickened his breath. Tonight would be a special evening. Earlier, he had tidied the house and emptied the remaining boxes to remove the stack from a corner of the living room. He switched on jazz music and, hands on hips, surveyed the results. "Looks pretty good, Dud."

Dudley wagged and panted.

"Thanks for your support." Evan rubbed his dog's furry sides.

He had encountered Jayne at the rec center on Monday but didn't get a chance to say more than a quick hello before the youth activities started. A huge frustration grew like a weed in his chest, because he couldn't greet her with a hug like he wanted. Other than that brief encounter, he hadn't even spotted her from a distance. Funny how their paths didn't cross in a town as small as Prairieville. She didn't avoid him on purpose, did she?

A few minutes later, a tap on the door announced Jayne and Sally's arrival.

"Come in." He swung open the door. Could she hear his heartbeats pounding?

"Thanks for inviting us. Dinner smells delicious." Shivering, Jayne handed over a salad bowl, slipped off her jacket, and surveyed the surroundings. "I like your place."

"It already feels like home. I hope you like Italian

food." He hung her jacket and waved her toward a comfortable chair. The aroma of melting cheese and oregano floated through the room.

Sally bounded in and immediately made herself at home, batting her tail and nuzzling Dudley.

"Perfect. I love pasta, and I brought Caesar salad. Do you need help with anything?"

"No, thanks. Just relax by the fire."

She settled into a chair and crossed her legs. The fire crackled and threw an orangey glow onto her face and the walls. He could hardly tear away his gaze. Girlish and alluring at the same time, she wore brown leggings and a gold top that hugged her shape and accentuated the light flecks in her hazel eyes. With her earth-toned outfit and rich coloring, she embodied autumn in a very attractive package.

Joined by Sally, Dudley leapt, nipped, and rolled on the area rug, and already, tufts of hair floated everywhere. "Enough, dogs. Out to the yard." Evan shooed the boisterous pair outside. He returned, rubbing his hands together. "Dinner will be ready in a few minutes. Let's hold our business meeting first, so we can enjoy the rest of the evening." He had promised her dinner as good friends, but his resolve weakened by the minute. He wanted to draw her close, bury his face in her hair, and kiss her sweet lips.

"Uh, sure. I guess so." Jayne shifted in her chair. "I assumed this whole get-together was business." She raised her voice into a question, then parted her lips into a smile.

Her eyes crinkled into amusement. He glimpsed the tips of her teeth.

"You start." She stiffened and leaned forward.

How could he steer his mind to business? Did she have any inkling of the way she sparked his feelings?

At that moment, the oven timer beeped.

He leapt up. "On second thought, let's eat dinner first." Something told him he better save the business conversation until later. Dinner might soften her mood.

"Good idea. I'm starving." Jayne followed and leaned against the kitchen counter.

He cut thick slices of lasagna and lit candles, leaving her to toss the salad. "Have a seat." He pulled out a chair opposite his spot and added Parmesan cheese and a basket of bread to the table. The spread transformed his place into his own Italian restaurant. His mouth watered at the scent of rich cheese, tomato sauce, and fragrant spices. In the flickering light, business concerns faded to the background. He settled into the date—at least, temporarily—he'd anticipated. Right now, he would savor the hearty food and her charming company.

"We could discuss options over dinner." She lowered her hands to her lap and glanced up from her plate.

"Let's wait and enjoy our meal first. Why mix business and pleasure? We have plenty of time for both." He had dined across from her before, but this time, he memorized every detail. He wanted her in his life—not as a good friend but as much more. She was the woman who would stand by him, no matter what, and never abandon him. Neck and shoulders tingling, he gripped his napkin and waited for her response.

"Okay, I guess so." She concentrated on her meal, avoiding his gaze.

Jayne's reluctance to postpone business talk was

understandable. She wore her determination to succeed like a spiky shell. Working for a non-profit organization, she had fewer resources from which to draw. She couldn't afford to spend more than the budgeted amount for the proposed expansion. Her concerns were justified. But did something else interfere with a meaningful, personal conversation? He passed the bread, and when his fingertips brushed hers, he felt a current of longing sizzle up his arm.

"How do you like living in Prairieville again?" She swept her gaze over his face.

"I belong here. Sometimes, I feel like no time has passed." He buttered a slice of bread. How could he eat? He was hungry, but the excitement in his stomach swirled too fast to welcome a meal. "Especially when I see someone like you, who is as familiar as ever."

She widened her eyes and sipped water. "I hope I've changed somewhat."

Apparently, she didn't take his comment as a compliment. "Only in good ways. You're more confident and even prettier than I remembered."

She bowed her head and covered her cheeks. "I've always been plain Jayne Jones. Just ask my mother." She shifted her gaze to meet his. "But definitely, I'm growing surer of myself."

"You're also womanly attractive. You were cute back in high school." A rush of heat, hotter than baked pasta, invaded his chest.

"Not exactly." She poked a bite of salad. "I was an ordinary, little mouse, and you insulted my teeth in front of the whole class."

"I did?" He nearly choked on sudden remorse. "I don't even remember, but I only bugged you because I liked you. What can I say? I was a dumb, awkward, teenage guy." How could he have acted like such a jerk?

"Really?" She quirked an eyebrow.

"*Really*." He leaned across the table and touched her hand. Her skin was smooth and gentle.

She hesitated, then flipped it over so her palm rested against his. "I wish I'd known."

Did wistfulness mellow her tone? "You know now."

"You called my teeth an *anomaly*. You have no idea how that comment, on top of my mom's ongoing criticism, impacted my life." Blinking, she swallowed and retracted her hand.

"I'm sorry." He wrung his napkin. As an immature teen, he'd had no idea the pain he'd caused. He wanted to hug her or, even better, kiss her and erase everything that hurt.

"You invited Melody to the graduation dance." Head downcast, she poked at her salad.

"She invited *me*, and I couldn't refuse." Laughing, he raised both hands.

Jayne shook her head. "Don't worry. Apology accepted." She paused and sipped water. "By the way, I forgave you for winning the top scholarship. I should never have written that essay and allowed you to submit it as your work." She shook her head and pursed her lips. "I was young and naïve."

He swallowed, and in a rush, memories squashed his insides. At the school award ceremony, guilt had nudged him at Jayne's crumpled expression and her mom's downturned lips. Now, he felt nearly sick with remorse. If he had not earned financial assistance to pursue studies in Toronto, how different life might have been. He blinked and met her piercing gaze. "The words *I'm sorry* hardly seem adequate."

She shook her head and softened her stiff expression. "Don't worry. High school is ancient history. I rarely think of those days. Like the message at camp, I strive to be kind and think well of people, no matter what."

"Thank you." With an exaggerated swoop, he mopped his brow. He didn't totally joke. Her forgiveness eased a little of the pressure in his chest. "Now, take my advice. Smile."

She set down her fork. "I will…when I get our situation…resolved." Then she flashed the barest hint of her teeth.

He studied her intelligent eyes, thin cheeks, and pink lips. "Okay, I'll hold you to your promise."

She nodded.

Hope invaded his chest. He would treasure the gift of a wide, genuine smile from Jayne.

"Do you keep in close touch with your mom?" She cut a bite of lasagna.

What made her jump to *that* question? He swallowed. She meant the mom who had raised, loved, and nurtured him all these years. "She likes life in Victoria. Golfs and plays bridge. When I call, I seldom find her at home." He wouldn't launch into the painful details of the outright rejection by his birth mother. Always lurking at the edges of his life, sadness tapped him on the shoulder. Maybe some other time. "Now for dessert. I hope you like chocolate."

"Everybody likes chocolate." She widened her eyes.

His assumption was correct. He rose and cleared their plates.

She gathered the remaining items, followed, and placed them on the kitchen counter.

He stood elbow to elbow with her in front of the sink, then rotated toward her side. Nearly touching, he breathed her presence until his nerve endings fizzed and his lungs might burst. "Thank you. Your cooking was delicious." She crept her gaze over and, in slow motion, faced him.

Heat rushed over him like he sat too close to the fireplace. He traced her lips with a finger. Should he? Could he?

She tilted back her head.

The yearning in her eyes said *yes*, and he eased his arms around her waist. Deep longing thundered in his chest. He brushed his lips over her cheeks to her mouth and then kissed her with an intensity he had only seen in movies. He belonged in her life. Surely, now, she must agree.

Chapter 16

In Evan's arms, Jayne whirled into a mysterious and delicious place. Her lips tingled, and the jazz music floating in the air around them riffed into her memory. Whenever she heard that piece, she'd remember this moment. She wanted to melt into his world and remain forever.

But what about the complications? What about the secret she still hadn't shared? She couldn't charge ahead. She didn't belong in his arms or in his life. Gathering her breath, she placed her shaky hands on his chest. Panic shot through her limbs, and she backed away. "I can't. Please...no..." She glanced left and right. She needed to escape. "I should leave..."

Pacing to the living room, she stared out the window into darkness. A streetlight lit a swath of sidewalk, and crisp leaves scuttled by. An ordinary autumn scene grounded an extraordinary event. The first would be repeated year after year forever, and the second could never happen again. What should she do? How could she help him understand?

"Please, don't leave, Jayne. I'm sorry. Since the moment I saw you at Brad and Mallory's place, I've wanted to kiss you. My high school crush waited in the wings all these years." He paused, then sighed. "I won't touch you again. I promise I'll give you space."

She spun but waited near the window. "The

problem is, I don't want to stay apart. But I know that way is best."

"It is?"

"Yes, it is. We face two, big stumbling blocks." She crossed her arms.

"Two? We just need to sort out the land issue. What else?" Widening his eyes, he flipped up his palms.

She shook her head. Trying to explain would only make the situation more awkward. She should tell him about Cara so that he knew the real woman behind the shield. But she couldn't. The words clogged in her throat, and her knees quivered. Nothing could change the past.

Of course, sooner or later, Evan might learn the truth from Brad or via the grapevine, and he could judge as he wished. Jayne was no different than his own birth mother. She had left her baby in someone else's care. Was she any better than Evan's birth mother just because she actively loved Cara and participated in her life? She'd still brought a child into the world she couldn't raise. No, even if she resolved the land issue, she could never unite with someone who scorned his birth mother. A confusing mix of hurt and indignation twisted her insides until they ached.

"I care for you, Jayne." He took two strides forward and stopped. He rubbed her arm.

She stiffened and blinked. "I joined you for a business meeting—not a date." Regret squashed her heart. He offered the strength and integrity she needed in a partner. If only things were different, she could build a life with him. Someday, maybe they could even expand their family and devote themselves to their own much-loved children.

His face and shoulders crumpled.

Sincerity and pain hid in the folds of his face, and she wanted to hug him and reassure him everything was okay. But she couldn't. "I'll stay for dessert and our meeting. But no more. I need to take Sally home as soon as possible."

"Dessert coming up." He returned to the kitchen and busied himself filling plates.

Catching her breath, she remained near the window, then crept back to her place at the table. She clasped her napkin and pressed it onto her lap to still her hands. The red-and-white tablecloth and flickering candles taunted her with the romance that could not blossom.

"Brownies, ice cream, and fresh raspberries, ma'am." With a flourish, he served loaded plates. "Complimentary this evening. Baked fresh, just for you." He grinned.

His smile was stiff and unnatural. She couldn't enjoy the scents of chocolate and fruit tickling her nose. Evan's former, jovial self almost reappeared, but his voice held a hint of uncertainty, and the sheen of his eyes dulled. He must feel the same shaken confusion. She could never erase the magic that just happened. With quivering fingers, she tightened her grip on her fork. She flipped her gaze between her food and his face.

He blinked and slightly parted his lips.

Now, she knew they were deliciously soft yet irresistibly firm.

"Tell me. Please. What is so wrong we can't be together?" He searched her face.

"I can't explain." An ache throbbed in her throat. "You wouldn't understand." Why was she so afraid of rejection? "Please, let's just finish dessert and hold our meeting." The sweet chocolate and rich ice cream overtook her taste buds and almost sickened her. How could she indulge in a treat and pretend nothing was wrong?

"If you insist, now you can make me work." He slid back his chair and cleared plates.

"Thank you. I couldn't quite finish, but everything was delicious." She had barely choked down half.

"I won't take offense at your leftovers." Hands full, he chuckled.

His laugh sounded hollow like any merriment had been ripped away. She chose the chair by the fire, the same place she had started this distressing evening. Only a little over an hour ago, she had been filled with nervous anticipation. Now, she quaked inside with a bittersweet memory and a sad reality. She inhaled a deep breath of air infused with burning wood and traced Evan's movements.

He plunked on the sofa opposite and sighed. "The agriculture equipment dealership plans to relocate. Their move will leave the current building vacant. A large yard could be repurposed into a dog play area."

She widened her eyes. "Really?" She hadn't realized the possibility existed, but his idea made sense. "What about office space?" How could she discuss something so ordinary? She should just tell him about Cara and deal with the fallout, but dread thudded like a rock in her middle. Her feelings were too strong not to care what he thought.

"Extensive renovations would be needed." He

shifted and rubbed the back of his neck.

"Did you check out options for the clinic?" She tilted her head. What if she could snuggle next to Evan on the sofa? How could she concentrate on business? Her hair swung softly onto her cheek, but she clamped her jaw. She would show him he couldn't take charge.

He swallowed. "I'll be honest. No. We agreed relocating the dog shelter was the best option."

"I agreed to consider the possibility." She crossed her arms and glared. Trepidation prickled in her stomach. No wonder he saved this conversation until after dinner. His one-sided solution just added more proof a relationship would never work. The mellow background music did nothing to relax the mood in the room.

"Sorry, I misunderstood." He crinkled his forehead. "But the option appears viable." He paused and glanced at the fire. "Tell me what you found."

"Don Larson is nearing retirement. He might cut back on his law practice and work from home. That change would leave his space vacant, but he can't commit right now. The florist plans to stay."

"Where do we go from here?" Rubbing his temples, he leaned back.

She stared at the flames and absorbed the warmth, but the heat didn't ease the mounting chill in her limbs. Her lips still tingled, and she wanted to both run and stay. He was the most infuriating combination of kind and threatening. His solution really wasn't so bad. In fact, it made better sense than staying and expanding—if the shelter could afford the option. She had always believed building onto the current location would be the most cost-efficient approach, but she wouldn't know until she reviewed actual quotes. If she agreed right now, she wouldn't need to spend more time negotiating with Evan. She could avoid him and just share brief, friendly conversations at youth events.

"Jayne, I'll work with you on this project." Evan gripped an arm of the sofa. "And I don't regret what just happened in the kitchen. I want to build a relationship with you."

She shook her head. Getting involved would be wonderful…if everything was different…if she didn't treasure Cara in her life…if he didn't harbor his own complicated feelings about adoption…if he didn't hold total disdain for his birth mother.

"Tell me what holds you back, please. You felt the same spark."

"I…" She blinked and ran a finger under one eye. "Please…don't ask any more questions. I have my reasons." A heavy fog descended and wrapped her in a damp blanket. She shivered, even though the fire crackled nearby. She could just confess the reason for her hesitance. But what if he judged her for choosing to give up Cara? What if her shame returned—the burden she had worked so hard to release? No question her heart and her self-esteem remained safer this way.

"I don't understand, but I respect your decision." He cleared his throat and focused his gaze on her face. "How do you want to proceed with the land issue?"

His voice lowered to a tone so quiet she could hardly hear. She clenched her hands on her lap. "If I agree the finances work, I'll consider moving the shelter."

"Done deal." He leapt to his feet and held out a hand. "I'll investigate and report details as soon as possible."

She huffed. "You don't need to do the legwork. I'm perfectly capable—"

"Let me help. Mayor Tommy asked us to work together." He leaned forward.

"Don't think you can take over." She glared at the firm lines across his forehead and his intense, blue eyes. "Never."

At the same time, Jayne shot out of her chair. She hesitated an instant and shook his hand. Warmth travelled up her arm to her face, and she dodged him and headed for the back door. "I'll call Sally and walk home now." She swung open the door.

Sally, followed by Dudley, romped into the room along with a gust of cold air.

"Take it easy, pups." She chuckled at their pure joy with not a care in the world. If only she felt the same. "Thank you for dinner." She smiled at Evan her old, stiff way—not because she feared exposing her teeth but because she fought tears over the bittersweet evening. "I enjoyed it. You *are* a good cook." She blinked to clear the moist gloss over her eyes. He was also very good company—pleasant to admire and an entertaining conversationalist, too. Of course, she'd never forget his kiss. It stirred her in a way that only happened in romance novels.

"Told you." Smirking, he threw back his shoulders.

Evan attempted to show a brave front, but his smile didn't rise to his eyes. "Come, Sally." She slung on her jacket and opened the front door. A blast of chilly air laced with rich autumn scents swept inside, and she glanced back for an instant. Evan's expression drooped and dragged her spirits even lower.

He held Dudley by the collar and half waved. "I'll crunch numbers and let you know."

Stomach rolling, she nodded and hustled down the front sidewalk. His downturned eyes and mouth mirrored the regret she masked. She would see him only to sort out business details and to lead the youth group. Maybe the pain in her heart would lessen over time.

****

Evan closed the door on Jayne and Sally and dropped to the floor to pet Dudley. Rejection and hurt weighed down his limbs and his heart. He had prepared dinner this evening with high hopes Jayne would return his affection. Everything was perfect with their common interests and a possible solution for the conflict over land. So, why did she push him away? He couldn't give up. Her rebuff—especially after the deep intimacy they had shared—knocked him off balance, like a blow to the chest. Another tear in his heart felt all too familiar. Rising, he tidied the kitchen and blew out the candles. He refused to extinguish his hope.

****

The next morning, Evan stared out the living room window at the deserted street and bare trees. The afternoon ahead loomed as empty as the hollow spot inside his heart. Just then, his phone rang, and anticipation jumped in his chest. Did Jayne call? He answered on the first ring.

"Mallory, Cara, and I are in the car on the way home from errands. You're on speaker phone. Want to join us at Sam's?"

The sound of Brad's upbeat voice chased away daydreams of Jayne.

"Please come for lunch," Mallory piped in.

"Uh, why not?" Maybe some company would soothe his battered feelings. "I'll meet you there." He poised his thumb to click off the call.

"I want Auntie Jayne to come, too."

Slightly muffled, the sound of Cara's high voice lilted over the phone.

"Sorry about the interruption." Brad chuckled. "See you soon." He ended the call.

Evan threw on a jacket. Would Brad listen to Cara and invite Jayne? "Sorry, Dud. I'll take you for a walk later." He dashed out the door, breathed the chilly air, and headed for the diner. He agreed with Cara. He'd be more excited if Jayne could join them, but maybe a little cooling-off period from last evening would help— as long as only temporary. His chest ached with loneliness, and he couldn't block the image of Jayne's brave attempts to broaden her smile. Her straight hair and tortoiseshell glasses added up to the perfect combination of serious and playful. A wide smile would add a bow to the package.

The air hung so clean and crisp, it carried the promise of snow. Within minutes, he arrived at Sam's at the same time as the rest. In the entranceway, he caught a whiff of burgers and fries. The atmosphere overflowed with noisy conversation and the aroma of sweet and savory brunch foods.

"Glad you joined us." Brad slapped Evan on the back.

"Thanks, buddy. Hi, Mallory. Hey, Cara." Evan bent and fist-bumped Cara. He felt a stab of envy at Brad's beautiful family.

"Hi, Evan." Smiling, Mallory squeezed Cara's

shoulder and, with her free hand, flipped back her hair.

"Hello, all you beautiful people." Louanne breezed over and encircled them in a group hug.

Was she everywhere? Brad didn't invite her to join them, too, did he?

"How lovely to see you." Louanne dropped her arms. "I'm seated over there with some girlfriends." She pointed to a booth filled with three other women. "Where's Jaynie?"

Suddenly, too hot in his jacket, Evan squirmed. He wished he knew. "I haven't talked to her today— unfortunately." He scanned for an empty table.

"Well, you better fix that little problem, mister." Louanne giggled and waggled her fingers. "Enjoy your lunch. I'll dash back to my friends now. Call Jaynie, Evan."

"Thanks for the idea." Evan shoved his hands in his pockets. Shrugging, he glanced at Brad and Mallory and laughed. With any luck, he sounded more upbeat than he felt. How could he change Jayne's mind?

Grinning, Brad jostled his arm. "Jayne *is* pretty nice."

"She's *really* nice." Cara bounced on her toes.

Her intense, little face poked out under a woolly, pink hat. She looked like a pencil topped with an eraser. With the clatter of dishes and buzz of diners, Evan was surprised she even caught the comment.

"I love her." Cara clasped both hands over her heart. "She's my birth mommy."

Evan widened his eyes and swallowed. Jayne was Cara's birth mother? A flood of emotion threatened to knock him sideways. Had she made the same choice as his own birth mother? Surely, he hadn't heard correctly.

He searched Mallory's and Brad's faces for confirmation or denial. Could the revelation be true? A little girl couldn't fabricate something that profound. Shock and confusion stormed into his chest and scraped the inside. Why had Jayne treated the truth like a secret? Didn't she trust him enough to share such an important part of her life?

Mallory exchanged a glance with Brad and smiled down at their daughter—their *adopted* daughter. "Yes, Cara. We all love Jayne. She is a very special part of our family."

"I gather you didn't know. I figured Jayne would share the details, eventually." Brad rested his hands on Cara's shoulders.

Evan shook his head. Why hadn't Jayne told him? She didn't need to be embarrassed. Sudden anger scattered inside him like tiny shards of glass—not because Jayne shared something in common with his birth mother but because she had held back such a significant piece of herself. No wonder Cara resembled her more than Mallory.

"Let's grab a table over there." Brad swooped an arm to a spot by a window. He glanced at Evan and lowered his voice. "I'll fill you in on the whole story later."

Evan followed the trio. Now, he floated on a wave of uncertainty. All his life, he had mourned being abandoned by his birth mother. When he first reached out, she had ignored his request and acted like he didn't exist. Finally, years later, she changed her mind. Hurt and angry, he refused to meet. Had he made a mistake? Cara thrived with two adoring mothers in her life.

Seated in a booth with the family of three, he

opened the menu and skipped down the list. Right now, he didn't care about food, but one thing was certain. He had an appetite to set things right with Jayne. He wouldn't rush, but when he had gathered the facts on a better option for Adopt-a-Dog, he'd arrange to meet. Then he'd broach the subject he couldn't wait to address. She handled a challenging situation in a mature, positive way. He would never criticize her choice, even if he scorned his own biological mother. The conversation might change their lives. Somehow, Evan chatted and joked with Brad, Mallory, and Cara and ate most of his clubhouse sandwich.

"Why don't you girls drive home? I'll walk with Evan." Brad grabbed the bill and hugged his daughter goodbye. "See you soon, sweeties." He glanced at Mallory.

She nodded and blew a kiss.

Evan welcomed her discretion. Now, he could learn more details in private. Was he a complete fool to have not guessed the truth? He needed to breathe and calm his racing thoughts. Outside, he drew in chilly air infused with the scent of burning leaves. Cara was *adopted*. Jayne no longer needed to hide her secret.

"We tried for years to have a baby. Healthy lifestyle, fertility treatments, the works." Brad set a brisk pace down the sidewalk toward his quiet, residential neighborhood. "We had all but given up when we made a last attempt at private adoption."

Evan's adoptive parents had desperately wanted a child, too. His birth mother had been young, single, and unable to raise him. Compassion for Jayne's tough decision squeezed from his stomach upward to his chest.

"Rumors trickled into Prairieville that Jayne was pregnant—at the time, she lived in Regina—and we connected through Iris. The first time Mallory and I met Jayne, we felt an instant connection. We promised to offer a stable, loving family and agreed Jayne and her parents would become active participants in Cara's life." Brad stared ahead. "When we learned the good news, we screamed with joy."

"Anybody can see how much Jayne loves Cara." Evan kept pace. He hunched his shoulders and flipped up his collar against the cold. The wind rustled dust across their path and cleared the way for winter.

"We're very fortunate. Jayne is a wonderful person. She supports us as parents, while staying involved as a surrogate aunt. Shortly after she gave birth, she offered us the gift of Cara. Within a few months, she moved back to Prairieville. Iris and Greg dote on Cara like any grandparents. We decided from the beginning, a child can't have too much love in her life."

Rounding a corner, Evan spotted his house down the block. "Thanks for sharing. Explains a lot about Jayne."

"Yeah. She's sensitive about the whole situation leading to Cara. We don't keep the nature of our relationship a secret, but we don't broadcast it, either. People in town either know and respect our privacy or aren't aware. We've explained everything to Cara. Normally, she doesn't blurt the details. Apparently, she wanted you to know." Chuckling, he shrugged.

"I'm glad." Evan paused at the end of his front sidewalk. "Thanks, again. See you at work." Now, he understood. Overwhelming relief lifted his spirits higher than the trees in his yard. Jayne didn't want to share her secret because she feared he would judge. He could relate because he wasn't perfect, either. She should feel proud and not embarrassed. He needed to let her know she didn't need to fear his reaction. Would she listen? He would never judge or turn against her. Would she believe the truth?

Chapter 17

A week later, at dinner with her parents, Jayne asked Dad for his opinion on an alternative location for Adopt-a-Dog. The aroma of baked chicken and roasted vegetables hung over the table in a mouthwatering veil. The table featured a cloth and napkins in rich, fall colors, and light music strummed in the background. Through the doorway to the front room, burgundy furniture and an area rug warmed the atmosphere. Challenging as Mom often was, she created a welcoming home environment.

At Jayne's feet, Sally lay positioned to grab any morsel that dropped.

"Why you want to expand your current location, I don't understand," Dad said. "You still won't gain the ideal amount of space. I learned on coffee row that the agriculture equipment dealership plans to relocate. The property suits the shelter. Would give you a lot more space—inside and outside. When you could grab another, probably better location, why fight the health center?"

Jayne listened carefully to her wise dad. "Why didn't anybody suggest that location sooner?" If she'd known of the immediate possibility, she could have saved much aggravation and lost sleep.

Dad sawed a piece of meat. "You didn't ask my advice. I wanted to support your plan. But recently, I racked my brain for options. You know how the town council operates. Sometimes, they share information on a need-to-know basis, or they avoid communication for confidentiality reasons. Who knows? Maybe you just need to ask the right questions to hear the right answers. Then again, maybe nobody connected the dots."

"Evan mentioned the same idea..." She pictured the sprawling building surrounded by open prairie. The location would meet the needs of staff, volunteers, and, most importantly, dogs.

"Makes sense. He shows a good head on his shoulders." Fork poised, he nodded and crinkled his eyes.

"Thanks, Dad. I'll check it out." She speared a bite of chicken and chewed. A combination of garlic and rosemary spiced it perfectly. Dad was always a voice of reason, and she trusted his judgment. If she proceeded down the path Evan had proposed, she couldn't go too far astray. Tomorrow, she'd decide.

"Speaking of Evan..."

Mom almost sang his name. A surge of attraction rose and fell like waves in Jayne's stomach. But she'd never give Mom the satisfaction of successful matchmaking.

"Louanne says you and Evan get along very well." Smiling, she patted Jayne's shoulder.

Feeling as awkward as a teenager, Jayne shrugged. "I like all the youth leaders." Blinking, she bowed her head to conceal sudden moisture. She wouldn't get drawn into this discussion. If things were different, she'd follow her heart right into his arms. But her past—and his opinion of his birth mother— were a wall too high to hurtle. She would always be kind, but her relationship with Evan would remain strictly friendship.

"Never say *never*, dear." Her mother glanced at her father and back. "He's a very nice man, and you're not getting any younger. You have a past, but you could still have a baby the *proper* way."

Jayne's mouth dried, and she sipped water. She inhaled a shaky breath, and from deep within, a force rose and jumped to her throat. She needed to end the constant knocks to her self-esteem. Already, she was a positive influence on local youth. She had faced the town council's scrutiny. If she could lead a major expansion project for Adopt-a-Dog, she could confront her mother, once and for all. "Please stop." She raised a palm forward like she halted traffic. "I know you mean well, Mom, but your continual reminders of my shortcomings undermine my confidence and my happiness. I need you to let go of the past and focus on the joy Cara brings." She wrung her quivering hands around the napkin on her lap. Mom probably wouldn't change, but she could no longer shame Jayne.

Dad flashed a thumbs-up. "Listen to your daughter, Iris."

Mom widened her eyes, pursed her lips, and rested her hands on either side of her plate. "I love Cara, but I'd like to become a grandma for real, with a son-in-law who makes me proud. Our family creates endless happiness. Right, Greg?"

"Right, Iris." He dug into his mashed potatoes. "Thirty-six, fun-filled years of marriage." He quirked an eyebrow.

Jayne ignored Mom's latest dig and chuckled at Dad's wry tone. "I'm glad you two are still in love, but I don't agree Evan is the right guy." She stabbed a bite of salad, and her newfound assertiveness untied the knot in her stomach. But she didn't believe her own words. Evan could be the man who changed everything.

"Of course not. But he likes you and realizes what an attractive girl you really are…" Mom smiled and passed a basket of buns. "Imagine if you accepted Aunt Patsy's offer. You'd finally get those pesky teeth straightened and belong on the cover of *Prairie Woman* magazine."

Jayne swallowed, set down her fork, and fisted her hands in her lap. She had dealt with her mother's comments about her crooked teeth since she was eight years old, and she would no longer stand for the humiliation. She didn't mind her own teeth one bit, and Evan's encouraging words echoed in her head. "I appreciate Aunt Patsy's generous offer, but I won't take her money to pay for orthodontics."

Mom narrowed her eyes.

Dad concentrated on cutting a chunk of potato.

She steadied her breath. Nervousness fluttered from her stomach up to her throat and batted at her words. She swallowed. Enough was enough. She refused to allow Mom—or anyone else—to drag her backward. She would embrace her life choices and her appearance like a mature, confident adult. "The lack of perfect, straight teeth does not make a person less attractive, except in your eyes." Deep resolve marched her words into a slow, firm line. "My teeth make me unique and interesting, and I intend to show them more often." She had practiced her new smile, and in time, it would become natural.

Dad raised his head and fixed his gaze on Jayne. He nodded and spread a slow smile across his face.

"Mom, please, do not mention my teeth or cringe when I smile ever again." She stared at her and didn't waver.

Tears welled in Mom's eyes, and she blinked and swallowed. "I'm sorry, Jaynie. I only tried to help. You are perfect in my eyes, and I wanted to make sure everyone else agreed."

"I don't care what anyone thinks." Jayne tapped her fork on her plate. Determination sped her heartbeats.

"You're absolutely right." Dad pounded a fist on the table, then picked up his water glass. "Here's to you, Jayne."

Mom nodded, hesitated, and raised her glass.

Jayne glanced at Mom and Dad and stretched her lips open into a full smile. Her relief floated as light and carefree as dandelion fluff. For years, she had needed to confront Mom, and the whole experience wasn't as difficult as she had feared. She pictured Evan cheering, and a powerful blend of gratitude and affection swelled in her chest. "Thank you." She sipped her water. "If Aunt Patsy has money she doesn't know how to spend, she could consider a donation to Adopt-a-Dog."

"Good idea."

Dad's booming voice signaled full support.

Mom paused chewing and shifted her gaze from Jayne to Dad and back. For the rest of the meal, she directed the conversation toward mundane topics.

Gradually, Jayne's heart rate slowed. The atmosphere relaxed, and her food tasted better with every bite.

The next day at work, she still rode the confidence surging throughout her entire body. Finally, she had stood up to Mom and earned newfound respect from both parents. With hands on hips, she swivelled and surveyed the crowded office. "Space feels tight in here." The faint odor of dogs drifted from the back. Whenever Jayne wanted to meet with volunteers, she borrowed a meeting room at the town hall. More than a handful of visitors at one time made the place feel as crowded as a full elevator. "A new facility would serve us best."

Evan understood and cared. Sudden clarity warmed her like a hug. She trusted and valued his opinion. She wanted to draw closer and work together...if only...

"I've said so for years, girl." Jangling bracelets, Tasha waved her arms at the compact area.

"Evan asked me to meet him at Sam's this afternoon so he can outline a proposal he believes will work." Jayne's face grew uncomfortably warm at the way desire circled her heart. From the back, yips and woofs floated through the doorway and reminded her why she had landed in this complicated situation in the first place. Never mind Evan. Compassion squeezed her chest. She needed to offer a better life for the dogs.

"I'd ask to come along, but somebody better hold down the fort around here." Laughing, Tasha raised her eyebrows. "Besides, I suspect Evan would rather meet with you alone."

"What would I do without you?" Jayne bowed her head and faced her desk to hide her blush. "Don't be too sure about Evan."

"Oh, no question." Tasha spun her chair. "Enjoy your *meeting*."

"I just want to get it over with, but I won't leave yet. See you in a few minutes." Jayne popped into the kennel area to spend time with the animals and volunteers. She inhaled the musky scents of dogs and kibble. The atmosphere was a tonic that both soothed and energized.

Soon, she would face Evan over a table at Sam's. A deep ache would accompany her—a longing she couldn't ease. His teasing manner, open expression, and relaxed manner were the puzzle pieces she missed, despite their differences. He wasn't perfect, but he lived comfortably in his own skin. Just being near him sent tingles throughout her body, and when he kissed her...he carried her away to places she had only imagined.

She worked along a row of enclosures, petted dogs, and doled treats. She laughed at a mutt leaping and spinning in circles. "Thank you for your help." She raised a hand to two volunteers cleaning kennels and refilling water buckets. The place already housed too many pets, and the demand for care never ended.

At 2:45 p.m., she returned to the office and left the noisy barks and earthy smell of fur behind. Washing her hands, she glanced in the mirror above the sink. She smoothed her hair and added a touch of lip gloss. Grabbing her jacket and notebook, she avoided Tasha's teasing stare. Anticipation flip-flopped in her stomach. She would seal a deal and proceed without more contact than necessary with Evan. "See you later." Jayne flipped up the collar on her jacket and braced herself for the autumn chill. The sun shone but no longer warmed the air to a gentle temperature.

"Have fun, girl." Tasha grinned and waved. "I can't wait to hear all the details."

"Sure thing." She ignored the innuendo, but

uncertainty fluttered in her stomach. No matter how difficult, she'd focus on facts and not feelings. She'd stick to pure business…if possible.

****

Settled in a booth at Sam's, Evan checked his watch. The sounds of lively chatter and clattering dishes mixed with a playlist of hits from the nineties. Today, he didn't recognize anyone and appreciated a chance to focus on business…and Jayne. He had half expected to bump into her on the way here, and she was now three minutes late.

He dropped a notebook onto the table and eyed the menu printed on a chalkboard next to the ordering window. The sweet aroma of cinnamon, chocolate, and sugar drifted from the kitchen. On a nippy day, the place was cozy and inviting. Normally, Sam's puffed wheat cake tempted, but today, he only wanted to sip ginger ale. He'd cover a lot with Jayne. He glanced at his watch again.

Just then, she arrived in a gust of wind. Her hair swept across her face. She brushed it aside and shook her head to jostle it into place.

Admiration and attraction filled his chest. Did she have any idea how much she belonged in his arms? She already lived in his heart. He smiled and waved.

Bringing a swish of cool, fresh air, she wove through the tables and settled on the opposite side of the booth.

"How are you?" He studied her face, and by her crinkled forehead and the firm set of her jaw, he knew he likely wouldn't see her new smile today.

"I'm fine, thank you. I decided." She threw off her jacket onto the bench.

"Whoa. Can I buy you a snack?"

She paused and glanced up at the menu. "Lemon tea, please. I need something hot."

He crossed the café, ordered, and returned from the counter with their beverages, set them down, and took a deep breath. "You were saying?" Her face was composed and firm. She wasn't the only one who had made a decision. He would lay his feelings on the table and let her know her past didn't color his wishes at all. In fact, he had gained a deeper respect for her inner strength.

"*If* I agree the budget allows, I'll accept your idea." She blinked and stared into his eyes.

The restaurant clatter faded as if someone had lowered the volume. The other customers transformed into a colorful blur. He zeroed in on only Jayne and her intense hazel eyes, peering through her glasses. She became more attractive every time he encountered her—not only her understated appearance but her fierce determination. "Good. My preliminary chat with the owner bodes well. Do you know Bruce Calvin?"

"Everybody knows Bruce. He's Mayor Tommy's cousin." She suppressed a smile. "Must have been a long chat. He talks even more than Tommy." She sipped her tea and peeked over the rim. "I need to ask a hundred questions. Should I start a list?"

"Fire away." Evan chuckled and shifted his gaze from her face to his drink and back. She drew him like a magnet. He needed to convince her she could trust him in business and in life.

"Has the building been appraised? What's the estimated value? How much will renovations cost? How soon could Adopt-a-Dog assume ownership?

Obviously, my concerns involve finances and logistics." She cradled her cup and inhaled the steam.

"All great questions that need research and analysis to answer." He gulped a mouthful of ginger ale. "I didn't want to overstep my bounds, so I didn't talk specifics. You're the project leader." He respected her position of authority and needed her to know.

"Thank you for your consideration." She flickered a smile, offered a slight nod, then crinkled her forehead.

Was she overwhelmed by the magnitude of what lay ahead? He wanted to stroke her hair and smooth away her concerns. "Bruce is amenable to further discussions. I told him you would decide next steps." Would she relax her fierce independence enough to let him assist? Was she too stubborn to accept help?

"I'll book a meeting, the sooner the better." She straightened and rested her forearms on the table. "Among all my regular duties."

He studied her expression. Did a hint of self-doubt muddy her hazel eyes? She was well aware of the immense task ahead. He wanted—no, needed—to ease her burden. "Would you consider…?" He paused and tapped a fist on the table. "Let me volunteer for Adopt-a-Dog and work side by side on the details. You can direct and delegate as you see fit. Will you agree to that arrangement?" He could spend more time with her and, at the same time, help his community.

"Really?" She widened her eyes, then furrowed her forehead until her eyebrows almost joined. "Do you understand the extent of your offer?"

In the background, Sam shouted an order. His announcement served as the only reminder anyone else was around. Evan focused on his private world with

Jayne. "I understand completely. I'd follow your lead."

She clapped a hand to her chest, paused, and stared out the window. "Possibly. Of course, I'm fully capable of handling the details, but I never turn down volunteer labor. Adopt-a-Dog can use all the support available."

"Deal?" He searched her eyes, and a velvet gaze coated with steel glistened back. He offered a handshake to seal their agreement.

"Deal, I guess." She shook his hand and almost smiled. "Thank you. *But* this arrangement is all business and not an excuse to spend time together."

His adrenaline surged. The solution worked for both projects, according to Mayor Tommy's wishes. Now, despite hearing Jayne's stern reminder, he had found another reason to spend time in her charming company. "I'll start tomorrow and keep you posted." He sipped his drink. He couldn't let her slip away before he told her what he had learned from Cara.

"Thank you. I really appreciate your help." She shifted, finished her tea, and fumbled for her jacket. "I need to get back to work. I'll let you know the next steps."

"No, please, wait." Apprehension forced his heart to pick up speed. He'd leap to the core of the matter that concerned her so greatly. He had criticized his biological mother without realizing Jayne was a birth mother, too. With good reason, she must feel rudely insulted and deeply hurt. No wonder she shunned his advances. The realization punched him in the stomach. He took a deep breath and opened his mouth.

Chapter 18

Bewilderment gripped Jayne and glued her to her seat. She dropped her jacket on the padded bench and leaned back. Evan's offer to assist with the relocation as a volunteer left her stunned. If he didn't care about the outcome for Adopt-a-Dog, he would never make such a generous offer. How could she refuse? She just needed to make sure their work dealings didn't cross into anything too personal. And now, he wanted to discuss something else.

Her heart beat like she just won a race. "Okay, but I can only stay a few more minutes." Did he want to discuss volunteer work? She had explained stumbling blocks to a relationship. Just because they agreed on a new direction for Adopt-a-Dog didn't mean the other insurmountable issue could ever be resolved. He had no idea what or why.

"I know."

His gaze travelled past her eyes into her soul. She swallowed. "Know what?" Instantly, she understood what he meant, but she needed time to think and wrap her heart in a protective blanket. Fear and relief spun so fast she felt slightly dizzy. Fighting to regain her equilibrium, she drew in a full and shaky breath. Now, she no longer had to hide, but she still faced his judgment.

"About you and Cara. You are her birth mother."

He scrunched a napkin and kept his gaze locked on her face.

"Yes." Pride and certainty crowded into her chest, leaving no space for shame. She had transformed a serious mistake into a beautiful gift. Adoption remained the right decision. Playing a big role in Cara's life meant the world, no matter what anyone else thought.

"Who told you?" She detected the tremor in her own voice. He *knew,* and yet, he still wanted to spend time with her. Did he not judge her as harshly as his own birth mother? Could she still dream of possibilities?

"Cara. Very matter-of-factly during lunch at Sam's, she told me she loves you, and you are her birth mommy. You should have seen Brad and Mallory drop their jaws. Later, Brad filled me in on the full story."

He *knew*. The realization replayed over and over. "Uh…" Her mouth dried like salt. The details were private. They were no one else's business, especially not Evan's. She had figured the grapevine would catch up with him sooner or later but not this early and, certainly, not with Cara's help. Even Louanne respected boundaries on the topic.

How unexpected that little Cara had been the one to divulge the truth! Jayne's breath caught in her throat. But why not? Sweet, innocent Cara didn't see complexities like adults did. She didn't understand life-changing choices. She only knew Jayne was a special part of her close, loving family.

Jayne's eyes welled at Cara's spontaneous show of love and affection. She cherished the same rich, deep connection. But still, for Evan to learn through Cara…

"Trust me, Jayne." He slid a hand across the table,

then retracted it before he touched her arm. "I admire you for working out such a positive arrangement."

"Cara brings endless sunshine into my life. But I still feel a murky mix of joy and sorrow over what I gained but what I lost." Her throat ached, and she swallowed a lump as big as a marshmallow. Blinking away moisture, she searched his gentle expression and read compassion. He didn't judge or criticize. "I'm sorry I didn't tell you at the youth retreat. I tried." She stared out the window for several seconds. "But I couldn't choke out the right words."

His gaze never leaving her face, he nodded. "I knew you held back but had no idea you wanted to share something so important. You can tell me anything. I want to know everything about you. *Everything.*"

His quiet tone and absolute integrity promised her secrets were safe. She forced a ragged breath and rolled her quivering lips inward like a seal. She opened and closed her mouth. Finally, she straightened and met his gaze. "After university, when I lived in Regina, I fell for the wrong guy. What a horrible mistake." Blinking her burning eyes, she scanned the diner. Thank goodness, the crowd had thinned, and the remaining customers were engrossed in their own conversations. She didn't need an audience. Pausing, she breathed the sweet scent of baking mixed with the savory hints of today's dinner special.

Evan nodded and sipped his drink.

"He flattered me into believing he cared. Back then, I was too naïve to spot his insincerity and other signs of trouble—until way too late. He liked to party hard, and he was allergic to commitment of any kind.

When he heard I was pregnant, he ghosted me the very next day. His rejection, my…predicament, and the shame of the whole mess nearly crushed my soul." She lowered her gaze and studied her fingernails.

"The selfish jerk." Evan clenched his jaw.

His quick anger in her defense felt comfortably protective. "I soon realized I was far better off without him." She glanced up. Evan's unwavering gaze urged her on. "But I was young, insecure, and poor—in no position to raise a child on my own."

"Of course not." He rubbed his forehead. "I understand."

His steady presence underlined his words. He *knew*, and he *understood*. "Mom suggested adoption, and I agreed to a private arrangement with Brad and Mallory. Much as I struggled with shame and loss, I found the best possible parents for Cara."

"You chose well."

Over the restaurant clatter, she heard calm, genuine reassurance in his tone. She drew in a full breath of the aromas of spicy chili and fresh cornbread. The combination would always remind her of this revealing conversation and the day her life changed. Outside of Tasha, she had never opened up this way. His soft eyes and gentle manner urged her to share. Now, she trusted him with her business plan, her secrets, her heart, and everything else.

"Don't be too hard on yourself. You're not alone." He ran a hand along her forearm. "I've misjudged people, too."

Did he mean his biological mother? "I doubt your mistakes caused such serious repercussions. But, finally, I'm at peace with my decision, my relationship with Brad and Mallory, and my role in Cara's life."

"You made the best of an overwhelming challenge." Leaning forward, he smiled and squeezed her hands. "I admire your strength and resilience. You should be very proud."

She squeezed right back, with a surprising urgency. "Thank you." His approval meant a lot. "When I realized you rejected your own birth mother and didn't want her interfering in your life, I knew you'd never understand about Cara." She sighed and cradled her warm mug. "I feared your judgment and the possibility of a setback." She blinked to contain sudden tears from escaping down her cheek.

"Now, you know better." He cleared his throat. "Please, change your mind. Believe me. When I learned the truth, my feelings only grew. You reversed what could have been a terrible situation into something very loving and nurturing. Cara gained a family and never lost you in the process. You surround her with love and enrich her life."

Jayne bit her bottom lip. "I try hard."

"Cara proves you're doing well. She's a beautiful, happy girl." Releasing her hands, he rooted in a pocket and offered a tissue. "Here. Before you drip."

"Good call. I might get messy." She heard the wobble in her voice, and almost smiling, she gladly accepted. His eyes always twinkled when he injected a touch of humor, but right now, did they glisten with moisture?

"Whew. Just in time." He gave a scant chuckle, then scrunched his eyebrows. "I respect your devotion and commitment. You're nothing like *my* biological mother, who showed up twenty-five years too late."

"I'm glad." He supported and accepted her, flaws and all. She'd never experienced such overwhelming relief. Dabbing her eyes, she filled with a lightness so breezy and bright she might drift right out of her seat. She didn't need to hide from anyone, least of all Evan. Basking in a new kind of happiness, she gazed into his eyes, as blue and soothing as two pools of water. She would never tire of the view.

Jayne blinked and peered at Evan through damp lashes. "I don't know your mom or her situation, but I wouldn't be surprised if her heart breaks a little every time she thinks of the boy she lost and the man you've become. Maybe you'll decide to give her a chance, after all."

"Maybe." He gave a single nod. "Thank you for helping me understand. Now, please, think about what I said."

She blotted her cheeks and nose and took a deep breath. "Thanks for ruining my eye makeup." Smirking, she scrunched the tissue and stuffed it into her jeans pocket.

"I don't mind a few streaks." Examining her face, he offered a weak chuckle. Thanks for using my last tissue." He quirked an eyebrow.

"I owe you." She giggled.

"Seriously, you've carved a special place in my heart, Jayne. Bigger than you can imagine." He clutched her hands and squeezed. "You are the one—the total package." He paused and fixed his gaze. "You should also know…"

"Go on." She sensed his hesitancy and gently prodded.

"My heart holds plenty of space for a baby of our

own, when the time is right. Or four." He raised his eyebrows.

"Ha ha." She shook her head. "Uh, let's start with one." His eyes brimmed with love and hope, reflecting her emotions like a mirror. Together, they would support each other and work through anything. She felt a tingle on her lips and spread them wide into a full, genuine, all-out smile. "I adore you, too, Evan. More than you know." A rush of heat sizzled from her middle, up her back, to her face, and she clapped both hands to her cheeks. In the midst of the hazy air of the diner, she embraced her future as never before.

Evan's love and support opened new, exciting possibilities. She wanted him to leap over the table and kiss her. She wanted to wrap her arms around his neck and burrow deep. Most of all, she wanted to build a married life with him and, very soon, open her heart to their own baby for keeps.

He slid off his seat and rounded the table. "I need to kiss you this instant."

"Now? Here?" She didn't possess the willpower to resist. She scanned the restaurant and glanced out the window.

Right there, on the sidewalk outside, Louanne paused, smiled, and waggled her fingers behind the glass.

The woman appeared everywhere and, within minutes, would report her sighting to Mom. But Jayne didn't care. Nothing could dissolve the sugar of newfound love. Smothering a giggle, she waved like a princess, tipped back her head, and embraced the delicious, burning touch of her sweetheart's lips.

A word about the author...

Margot Johnson writes feel-good stories about dreams, family and romance. She is the author of three romance novels and three novellas.

Before focusing on the fun writing life, Margot held leadership roles in human resources and communications. She lives in the Canadian prairies with her husband.

Get in touch with Margot on social media.

Website: margotjohnson.ca

Facebook: AuthorMargotJohnson

Twitter: @AuthorMargot

Other titles by this author:
Let It Snowball, Book 1, Merilee Tours
Let It Melt, Book 2, Merilee Tours
Let It Simmer, Book 3, Merilee Tours
Love Leads the Way
Love Takes Flight